# SLAVE TRADE

# Books by Herbert Gold

# SLAVE

## a novel

# TRADE

## by Herbert Gold

ARBOR HOUSE
NEW YORK

Library of Congress Catalog Card Number: 78-73862

ISBN: 0-87795-217-5

Manufactured in the United States of America

# Slave Trade

In the service of God one can learn three things from a child and seven from a thief.

From a child, learn (1) always to be happy, (2) never sit idle, and (3) cry for everything you want.

From a thief, learn (1) work at night, (2) try again the next night, (3) love your fellow-thieves, (4) risk your life even for a small thing, (5) don't attach too much value to things just because you risk your life for them, (6) withstand all beatings and trouble but remain what you are, and (7) believe what you are doing is worthwhile, insist on it.

DOV BAER, the Mazid of Mezeritch

For Rex and Rita,
bringers of cheer

# Part I

I A fellow knows his own door on Princess Street and
doesn't examine it before entering. But even my front
door—wood and glass, from the time when security
was not the first thought—told me everything was now different. The nicks and splinters of Poorman's Cottage had
been supplemented by additional nicks and splinters. I
couldn't see just where, but I felt it. A man who lives alone
may not know himself but he knows his own front door.

I tried it. The door was closed, but unlocked.

It was near one in the morning. The curving street was
silent except for cats hunting true love and a pet chicken
clucking in the next house and the hum of Mission Street
down below. I had been hunting the same thing as the cats
and felt sympathetic to their problem. The chicken belonged to a Mexican kid. This was a San Francisco rural-
urban slum of Chicanos and blacks and toothless beatniks
and a few sixties hippies who had come back from going
noplace. And I opened the door and entered my own
house, feeling it was a stranger's.

I switched on the light and the girl, the girl, the girl in
the chair was alive, bound to my chair, and not screaming.
Little choking, peeping chest noises came from her mouth.

3

It wasn't a chicken after all. I wasn't very alert, but now I was. She was wearing faded blue jeans below, nothing above. She was pretty, though I like straight blond hair and hers was that kinky-curly they now seem to find ethnic and nice. Her chest was pulled tight against my towels. There was a red freckling which reminded me of the explosions of love, but it was only abrasion against the towels. I untied the towels and said, "Who are you? What happened?"

She was still clucking in that chickenish way. She reached for a pad of paper and wrote, *Mute.*

"You can hear okay?"

She nodded.

"I'll get you a shirt."

I went into the bedroom, cursing the luck that brought me this just when I had finally worked through my insomnia enough to think of sleep. I banged my shin on my footlocker. Why does a man settled as a civilian for all these years still use his army footlocker? When the Salvation Army could sell me a dresser? Just sentimental, I guess. And god gave man shins to find his footlockers in the dark. Another step; another scar.

A shirt, unironed, blue, work.

"Hey, put this on."

The chair was empty. My front door was open. The girl was gone.

I hobbled outside to find my garden quiet. Eilanthus tree, junk flowers, withered tomato plants, beer empties, and a stack of newspapers neatly tied in twine because I'm basically your good, nonlittering citizen. I lifted my foot to the soggy heap, rubbed my shin with my palm, and looked up and down the street. A black man in a cream-colored linen suit, broad-brimmed white felt hat—but somehow not a pimp, my intuition told me this, even if it neglected to remind my shin about the footlocker—tipped his hat and passed on down toward Mission Street. He was carrying a sleazo vinyl briefcase with the words Aeroport Son Excellence Dr. François Duvalier embossed on it in blue and red. He was in no hurry.

How did he know I was watching him, trying to register him in the meat computer forever? He turned and lifted his hat in a miniature toy bow. Hair shiny and straight, deep-fried conk. Ears pinker than anything but a seashell. He beamed toward me a smile of total innocent delight, teeth large, irregular, yellow, strong. I was thinking: Try to be a human Polaroid. As in the old days, try to remember all this.

He didn't seem to mind. Perplexity was alien to his spirit. He lifted his open palm to his mouth and licked it and then blew me a kiss. Must be a stranger in town, wanting for friends. I really couldn't help him. He finished his little performance, which was the opposite of incognito, and walked on. He was a man with a plan, but not a care in the world. He didn't even mind what happened to his plan. I had seen enough of his tongue, dripping raw meat, to recognize it in a tongue line-up.

Princess Street, tonight, outside my door was more ethnic than usual. This was the kind of evening that tends to make me lonely. Also finding lovely mute girls tied to my chair makes me feel uneasy, especially when they disappear without a real good-bye.

The man had something to do with the girl, but since he was acting like a bobbing lure attached to the cruel hook, I would act like the cautious, bruised, scaly old fish which, in fact, I am.

2 The last woman to visit Poorman's Cottage, before the swift mute, was my former wife and best friend, and that was nearly a year ago. She had come to seal with a kiss her retirement from both wifely and best friend activities. "I would like to say I still care for you," I said.

"You may say it."

"And if I still love you?" I asked.

"You may not say it. But you will get over it. Everybody does. And it's not like you to treasure a total loss forever, Sid." She put her coat down on the chair and began folding over it, in proper order, blouse, skirt, panties.

"Goodwill?"

"What?"

"This nice old chair from Goodwill?"

I nodded. Not necessary to tell her the price.

"Make some other friends," she said. "Meet some interesting people. This floor is cold on bare feet, so if we can stop discussing—"

She had a plan for her farewell. All the legal business was through. There was something pure in this visit which appealed to her. It could mean everything to me and nothing to her. Or it could mean everything to me and some-

thing I would never understand to her. Or it could—
"You're thinking, Sid. Stop this at once."
She drew me close. She wanted to wake me from my nightmare of total loss. She got busy. My chief activity was metabolic—fright, pain, regret, heat radiating and my heart loudly straining.
She put her hand on my chest. "My god," she said, "but you're making a noise inside. Don't overwork, darling. Here, let me help."
She blew hot breath against my chest; it dried the sweat; it was a bath of breath. Oh, this pleased me. She was an original creation, tongue on my shorts, in the fly of my shorts, breath then blowing again. This playfulness was serious.
I was once a boy filled with blood in the Richmond District, a lover filled with hope. I had learned to douse the feeling because it always brought me back to my wife and that hurt too much. This was better.
"Shush, baby."
Oh, better.
Her tongue on mine (much better than thinking), her tongue all over me, her tongue greedy and making me greedy for more. I would pay the penalty tomorrow if necessary, thinking again with that sick lurch of loss: my dear, my dearest.
Just then it felt just fine.
And tomorrow I would think again about my grief and the grief of that wife I still loved, who loved me no more, whom I hated, who didn't love me, who had no need to think of me. (That was my old life, she once said, now I have a new life.) She had been a chill creature with the griefs of her chillness. We had warmed each other awhile. She had thought to look in dreamland for the perfect prince with the distinguished profile. Perhaps I merited her scorn, for profile anyway. I got it.

7

A smile and her eyes glinting with as much crazy as she ever showed—not much crazy. "I'll stop thinking if you will," she said.

"Deal."

So no use in waiting for her. She was going no further with me on this ride. I thrust myself alone into obscure and meaty regions. I might never see her again. I might never touch her again. This could be entirely for me. At the other end of me there moved and breathed what's-her-name. At the end of care, giving up, I penetrated Priscilla as if it were the last time. She intended it to be the last time. Her knees flew up like a construction alongside my flanks. Something in her throbbed like a clock of meat. My wife, my former wife and best friend, that dry lady screamed.

What do we know? What do we know?

Then we dressed and drank cold coffee. I had learned to like cold coffee from her. "Well," she said. "Should I have a vet send you a dog or a cat?"

"Only cooked. I don't plan to take care of animals."

"That's how I felt about you, Sid. I don't want a husband, a kid, or a hamster. Nothing personal."

"I try to understand that."

"It might even be my loss, Sid, but no point in hashing through all that again. It was nice seeing you this afternoon, and if it weren't so dangerous—"

"We could see each other again."

She shook her head slowly. Such was not the plan.

I knew her politeness. She was so polite it bordered on courtesy. We had taken care of legal matters. Equally she had disposed of personal matters, such as that we once loved each other. She was cheerful and efficient and did good works in hospitals. It was her telephone manner. "Good-bye, good-bye, good-bye forever," she said cheerfully, "and good-bye again. I hereby release you—"

"Thank you. I can handle that myself."

"Oh dear, that sounded rather weird, didn't it? But you stopped me too soon. I hereby release you from all obligations. There!" she said, and sank a peck of packaged kiss onto my cheek.

"I'll remember you," I said.

"I release you from that, too."

"It's not in your control."

"Oh well. So good-bye. That's your decision, Sid."

"I'll not forget."

"You have grown into a way of nagging at things, dear. You didn't used to, when we first met."

"You remember when we met?"

"You see? You see? You're doing it again." She was completely dressed and at the door and ready. She stopped her fidgeting. "Okay, I remember. I really do. That's what I've been trying to tell you. I came to tell you, Sid. So good-bye."

I waited. Nothing comes after good-bye, does it? She deeply meant this good-bye. I assented.

In the vacant space of Poorman's Cottage, before the mute girl appeared, I had grown to know through the ending of my marriage that I am fantastic at predicting the future. I am very strong at it. Trouble is, I can't make the future match my predictions. For a year I lived off regret and savings, no love and no work, discharged from both. I confined myself to trying to predict the past, about which I thought I had adequate knowledge. I collected my pension for eighteen percent disability, up from eight percent due to straight-through-the-heart hangdog looks I gave the V.A. examiner one foggy December late afternoon in the Presidio. I told him my absent toe hurt from the damp and mentioned the mudslog of Korea, being careful not to make jokes, and wore my shabbiest private-eye grayman disguise, and remarked I was temporarily out of employment. But I think the operative function was that I looked as if I was just going to sit and sit there, peeking at the papers on his desk and peering anxiously into his eyes, and he just wanted to get back to his coffee and his Sporting Green of the *Chronicle*. When I left him I went for a little run under the redwoods to get rid of the nasty metabolic deposits left from my cunning imitation of a whiner.

What really hurt, hurt me all the time, worse than a missing toe—and no U.S. Army pension for this—was a missing wife. Was the nagging nerve ache that I must have let Priscilla down by not insisting on having a child, not insisting she be a woman—by letting her remain a girl as she turned thirty. I loved her like a mute hangdog and she thought I was a swaggering nine-toed toughie. I wanted to be her baby tonight and every night. It must have felt nice for a girl. She grew a little older. We didn't tell each other our secrets. In her loneliness she turned into a kind of wounded beautiful woman, the sort of thing a clever old girl does when she doesn't know how to do it. Eventually she saw the years with me stretching ahead like a row of tract houses in Daly City, while all her juices ran toward dreams of white horses, turreted castle, romance. And a fresh rider on that white horse.

I was out of work, a retired intelligence man, a defrocked private investigator.

I could do nothing, nothing, and nothing again about the wife I had loved.

It took events from outside Poorman's Cottage and Sid Kasdan's head to teach me what to do when pissing into the wind: Turn around, please.

**3** I lost my license as a private investigator because, essentially, I didn't want it. Oh, that's not the whole story. I'm passive enough and made them take it away from me. A stupid bust for more grass than I strictly needed for myself. But if I were really dealing, would I live like this? Not a Ferrari or even a Porsche; not a hell of a lot of equipment unless you count a dry mop; not a draft from a Swiss bank anyplace in my cottage. I looked and smelled to myself like a Korean veteran who was still struggling to stop being a boy.

Probation.

Reduction to Misdemeanor 404-J—Middle-aged Acting Out. But my investigator's license was suspended and I decided to postpone the appeal until I was young again.

Now I wanted to do more than hang out in San Francisco. I thought I might use my insomnia, grief, and typewriter to become a writer. I kept a journal, trying to remember what I did. But now I couldn't sleep again, didn't feel like writing, felt like giving real life another try, and wondered what a mute girl thought she was doing tied up in my itchy Goodwill mohair chair. And why she left without saying good-bye.

11

After I battened up the front door, I fixed all the windows as best I could to make sure nobody returned through the climbing vines. I didn't want sooty Santa down the chimney either. I didn't like these Halloween tricks during the balmy days of a San Francisco September. I sat where the girl had sat and waited for the phone to ring. You might have expected a squirmy smell where a girl had been strapped in, but there was a sweet, picklish scent of some kind of perfume she had left behind.

After awhile, as I knew it would, the phone rang. It was now nearly two a.m. "What do you want?"

"Sleeping?"

"Get to it."

"This is Sid, isn't it?"

"And this is the chap who ties up quiet skinny little blond eighteen-year-old ladies, isn't it?"

"She's twenty." Twunny, he said. "I wish to talk with you."

"You got a nice way of introducing yourself."

"I want you to listen."

"First you explain, then I listen." I rubbed my shin. If the girl was an attention-getting device, I didn't need any such.

"I wish you to realize we are serious and extreme."

"That was a psychotic stunt."

"You are not going to listen?"

"I'm not sure."

"Lots of money."

"If what I wanted was that, I might have had it by now. High IQ. I could have used the GI Bill to learn a decent trade."

"Fun and excitement."

The fellow was playing my game: teasing. I was trying to place his voice. I didn't know him. There was an accent, an intonation. The voice had mangoes in it. The accent had a sugary edge. Yet his American was perfect except for a little too much caution. "You write recruitment posters? ... Travel and kill lots of interesting people? I've turned down people I *know*, man."

"So I am different. But I am willing to get acquainted. May I come to visit now?"

"Alone?"

"I shall bring the girl you have already met."

I tried to imagine the months and years ahead, and as soon as I did so, I remembered the sinking feeling in my stomach whenever I performed this act, only now I didn't have it. Something was happening. Yes, I would see them. But I would not let him know how desperate I was to get going again.

"I'm tired," I said. "Whatever you got in mind, I only have conversation in mind and I need my sleep to keep up with you. How about tomorrow night about eight? You bring some take-out and we'll have dinner at my place."

"Take it out for three," the calypso voice on the wire answered cheerily. That's it, Caribbean, Rastafarian, those were the mangoes and papayas and I didn't quite have the sweetness in that voice placed yet. "Twenty hours precisely," he said.

He beat me to hanging up. I didn't mind. I yawned. It was nice to go to bed with a sense that the empty bag was about to be filled. Something happening. I slept with no dreams I can remember and woke with no thought of what's-her-name.

**4** It had just gotten dark. That was a mistake on my part. If I had said seven, and they were there promptly at seven, I'd have had a look at them in daylight. They got there promptly at eight, but the lingering musky gray in the air required electricity. Their smell was okay, however. Thank god, no ribs or pizza in those bags and boxes. Chinese. Good.

The girl had learned to talk in the intervening day. And she was not *twunny*, either—too smart. So they lied a little. She set a table because we didn't feel like a picnic on the floor near my slagpiles of records, boxes, newspapers. I'd removed the stranded socks and towels. She was one of those ladies who knows where to find the stainless steel-ware and the teapot. They had brought chopsticks. I was a guest in my own house.

I remembered him, of course, although he didn't have his black vinyl briefcase with Aeroport Son Excellence Dr. François Duvalier embossed on it. He meant for me to remember him. He noticed my eyes on his face and lifted his palm to his mouth in that little kiss-blowing gesture. "As a North African Arab, though I look black, I am actually as Semitic as you are, Meester Kasdan, although your name—"

"You may call me Sid at dinner."

"—but I must finish. I am part Syrian, born in Jeremie."

"Jeremie?"

"La république d'Haiti. Of wholly noble mother whose ancestors come from Dahomey."

"Thank you very much."

"For what? This description? Ah, I see. I say the ancestors of my mother come from Dahomey because such is the fixed reality of my life. Forevermore they come from Dahomey."

"There's a woman I feel like that about, too."

"Mahmoud Fils-Aimé is my name. I thank you for your confidence in me."

"I have none."

"Mais vous êtes accueillant quand même. Tu parles français?"

"La plume de ma tante," I said.

"Mahmoud is your friend and guide," he said, "but not your chief. However, the appetites come first, and then we shall talk."

"You too are hospitable, my man Mahmoud," I said.

All the while he was talking, we were talking, it was just talk so I could get used to him. He had done his work on me already. He must have been watching me these months. He had looked into my case. He knew what he wanted from me. He knew how to handle people. Open-collared white shirt, blue blazer, shiny conk, English shoes, clean-shaven with little pink razor nicks like the pink of his ears. He seemed too straight to be either a narc or a dealer. Was someone in the habit of picking him up by those ears? But probably he was a dealer in some kind of old-fashioned con, I thought; and that turned out to be a pretty good guess, although it was a new one on me. He had a nice funky baritone. It was French Caribbean mango, not English. The girl worked as efficiently for him as if she had come from the Helping Lady agency. She looked better with clothes

15

on, as girls sometimes do. The hair didn't look so outrageously frizzy.

"You use chopsticks?"

"Always," I said. "Steel conducts the heat and cold against my teeth. Yucch. I even eat my poached eggs with chopsticks."

"We gonna have to deal with your smartass talk?" the girl asked.

"I had to deal with your not talking last night."

"Well, we wanted to get your attention."

"You have it. I don't want trouble. I don't want to be a mule. I don't enforce debts. I don't pilot planes or boats. I don't serve as bodyguard. I don't blackmail or stool. There are things I do, but right now I don't know what they are."

I did not enjoy the thought that while I had not been sleeping very much, fretting away the days and nights, thinking only of my wife, this Syrian African Haitian gentleman had been thinking about me and how I could serve. I didn't know how I could serve, so how could he know?

"We understand perfeckly," he said in that sympathetic and kindly baritone—a little lilt in it—"and it is rather rare to find a private detective with your qualifications, very unusual, even somewhat intelligent, in addition to time hanging heavy, and speaking French besides, is it not? You understand our position."

"Not at all."

"I mean simply that we might go to considerable trouble to engage your attention. You might not believe if we brought a proposition and said it is unique in our world. But now you may listen and you may even think we are serious."

"I gather you are not trying to entrap me."

A calypso smile broke over that solemn, pouting mask. "Only in the deepest possible sense, sir. And where did you learn your excellent French?"

16

"I learned my mediocre French with the French army in Viet Nam. They still called it Indochine. It was the next best thing to joining the Foreign Legion for a crazy kid after Korea. I'm sure you know that."

He gazed winsomely at his reflection in his shoes. "Mon cher," he said.

The girl looked up. "You don't have any soy sauce, crazy kid?" she asked. "They forgot the soy sauce."

"In Indochine, we used a rotten-fish sauce. All the best rotten-fish restaurants were called Cordon Bleu."

"You see," said my sympathetic visitor, "we are just nice friends. Sid, call me Mahmoud and this is Five. Use ketchup if there is nothing else. Some people know, but nobody *really* knows how tasty all-brands ketchup on Cantonese food."

"Really à la carte," I said. "Listen—Five? You named after Saint Five?"

"She said she only enjoyed in the carnal sense five men before she met me."

She looked at him with a certain gaiety. Ah, youth. "Now you can call me Five-and-a-Half. My name is Luci."

We ate pork fried rice, egg rolls, shrimp in hard crust, tomato beef (with ketchup), chicken chow mein. They had clearly not picked from the à la carte menu. They had walked into the Chinese Kitchen and asked for dinner for three, deluxe, which is not how your gourmet take-out stylist normally operates. I didn't need to join the clean plate club for these folks. "What's on your mind?"

He picked at rice, a grain at a time. Mahmoud was chunky, heavy, like a Samoan swimmer; Luci was skinny; neither was a really good eater. As if I were already in their hire, they were trying to force me to speak first.

"I would guess it has to do with narcotics."

He was silent.

"I won't do it."

I was silent. Finally Luci spoke. "It has to do with people," she said sweetly.

"And I'm a people person?"

"It has to do with money," Mahmoud said.

"Many things come to that."

"But you do not really care so much about money."

"Most people don't, really."

Luci nodded as if she understood this conversation.

"You speak French. You are independent. You have a certain quickness which is unused. You are bored."

"I qualify in all those ways," I said. "But I won't be a mule. I don't want to go to prison in the latter half of my life. Time outside is bad enough. I don't want to exaggerate it."

Luci spoke up, and I knew Mahmoud wasn't just using her because I would listen better to Luci—that vision of the lost waif tied with towels to my chair, and the picklish smell she left behind. She hadn't merely been fed the explanation. She understood it all the way through.

They wanted me to go to Paris. I wouldn't have to carry anything, going or coming. They just wanted me to look into a situation. There were risks for their group which they personally didn't want to assume. They would prefer for me to assume certain chances and onerous duties. (His face pursed together in a pout of careful business. There was a thickness. He put a finger in his mouth, sucking up his thought. He wanted to admit very little, yet keep me engaged.) On the other hand, he was saying, I personally would receive certain rewards: money, of course, plus other pleasures . . .

Later they would explain in detail everything I needed to know, yet not enough to burden me. I could travel light. My passport hadn't expired.

"I told you I don't want trouble."

"We told you we know you need some business because you're going ass over bats with boredom otherwise."

18

"Occupation is one thing, Luci, trouble is another."

When Luci caught me looking, really looking at her, the hard and elegant childface suddenly softened, she blushed, it took on the dramatic smile—lips slightly curled to show teeth, profile turned, eyes regarding carefully noplace—of a pretty young woman who notices that she is being admired. She was acting; she wanted to please a man whom she was also willing to wipe away if he gave her any trivial difficulty. I might give her enough important difficulty to wear out my welcome and use up my credit. And yet she fell into an old way of receiving admiration from this man, just as if I didn't remember her smell on my chair and that was all. I remembered my wife's tongue expertly searching out the places of special pleasure.

In another life, I could imagine Luci fleeing Mill Valley for a safe home in the inner city ghetto of Chicago.

"Luci Worthington," she said, "with an i. Pretentious, but you'll remember the name. It's a family business. Now listen, listen pretty good. Here."

She handed it to me while Mahmoud discreetly looked away and I opened the envelope.

"This is a first," she said, "me paying you."

A stack of hundreds.

"For your first expenses," she said. "And for your suspicious nature. Be consoled. We are serious."

I looked at her, at the money, at Mahmoud, at her. And back to the stack of hundreds. I think I grinned. One feels sheepish, taking money from a pretty thing. I kissed her cheek. "You have bought my love," I said.

"I don't think so, but I doubt it," she said. "You didn't kiss the right place. But at least you know that what you don't know is interesting."

I nodded. Well put.

"There is also an airline ticket and a hotel reservation card. I think you'll find everything in order."

"Not everything," Mahmoud said.

19

"Use your good sense and pay attention," she said.

They knew enough about me to know that in due course I would pay attention. They didn't burden themselves with information about my soul or the weather report. This was a good sign. The money was an excellent sign. Since they were smart and smartly focused, why shouldn't I ride awhile?

They had my attention.

**5** I was on a Pan Am flight over the pole from San Francisco to Paris. This way there is no stop in New York, and although you arrive with a horrible case of the jet lag, jet forward, your brain mashing mushily against one end of your head because it floats in its fluids more stubbornly than the plane flies, you do miss the stopover in New York. So you pay for missing New York with a few extra million lopsided brain cells. Win some, lose some. Going along with my man Mahmoud and Luci Worthington meant I had some curly brain cells to start with.

I had been told to check in at the Hôtel Madison, Room 57, at St.-Germain-des-Près. The room was reserved in my name and they treated me like an old client. "Ah, monsieur"—that intimate French commercial enthusiasm. In fact, like Mahmoud and Luci, they seemed to know me. A headache you wouldn't believe. Perhaps it was from just thinking about my "quick"—they called it—brain pressing lopsided against the back of my skull while the 747 hustled at five and a half hundred miles an hour toward Charles de Gaulle Airport. Leave me alone until I sleep it off, I prayed to my friends back in San Francisco and my new unknown friends here in Paris, I have this delicate cranial beanbag.

Dark enough in the room. Dark stained wallpaper, drip in shower, no more flower smells and bird cheeps in inner Paris. The boulevard St.-Germain outside my window, past the statue of Diderot giving his raised finger to the church, sounded like Mission Street at rush hour. Motorcycles, mufflers removed, and the laser whistles of cops telling the traffic to do something different. Three aspirins. I slept.

When I awoke, the buzzer by my bed was ringing. Someone to see me.

"What time is it?"

"Should we send your breakfast up?"

I gathered it was morning.

The breakfast tray was delivered by a Norman lady with a permanent vin rouge sunburn. She uttered a jolly "Alors!" followed by a "Voilà, monsieur!" The tray was crowded. Two sets of everything—cups, croissants, butters, sugars, and a large pitcher of milk and coffee. Oh, that would be good. But evidently I was expecting a guest for breakfast. I sat up in bed and felt my head. It was numb, but more from the aspirin than the headache. Good. It could deal with other people's plans for me.

The door opened and my company entered.

This time it was Sid Kasdan, the hairy defrocked eye, who was naked in a place, but I wasn't surprised to have a visitor and I wasn't tied to mohair and therefore the deal was not symmetrical.

"Bon jour," said Luci.

"Shit. What kind of games?" I asked.

"Have your coffee, don't you like French roast? It's better than Chinese Kitchen take-out," she said.

I poured half a cup of milk, then darkened it with coffee, starting cautiously. "I thought you promised I didn't have to kill anyone, do anything illegal like that," I said.

"We promised," she said.

22

"Or run excess risk of getting killed myself," I said.

"We did have such a conversation."

"Then why are you here?"

"To make sure you got here A-okay and won't goof off."

I winced. Next she'd go into a Roger-and-out riff. The girl was barely born, if that, when I was in Indochina and Korea and she was still using World War II slang. "Keep on truckin'," I said, "and it ain't you, babe," but she ignored this, which was clever of her.

"I'll get out of your way pretty soon," she said. "The people you need to see are in the Hôtel des Trois Portes, rue Xavier-Privas, right off the rue de la Huchette."

"I could have all that memorized."

"You just have to make them know you. Smartass a little. Don't threaten, just be your American threatening smartass self. Hang out. Don't carry any weapon at all. Talk fast if you need something offensive. Wear a watch. Tell jokes. I don't care. Mahmoud doesn't care. Make them know you're around, available, but don't do anything remarkable. You're just gradually working up toward being a special person, Sid."

"I know. I remember. Why are you here?"

"And now," she said.

The level of coffee had gone down. My mouth felt a little sweeter after swallowing a few times. She was removing the tray from the bed. She was slipping beneath the covers. She was slipping out of her English tweed skirt, her English cashmere sweater, and was just hugging me. A cuddle, a top of the morning stretch. I hadn't yet touched the hair on her head. I was feeling the soft aura of hair on her arms. The softly bristly hair below. Now I touched the hair on her head. She had ironed it straight and I hadn't noticed.

"Welcome to Paris," she said.

"You have a nice way of curing the jet lag."

"You think I don't have the same problem?" she asked sweetly.

An hour later I inquired if she was planning to hang around and take care of me and supervise. She said she was going back to San Francisco tomorrow and wouldn't be seeing me again. She asked if I believed that. I said I didn't believe and I didn't disbelieve. I was going to let be what will be.

"Good fellow," she said.

"Not for nothing did I live through the groovy sixties," I said.

"You call what you did living?"

"What I'm doing now I kind of like, however."

"Good fellow. I hope so."

I might carry some things. Depends on what. A person in my condition has to measure risk against money, pain against fun. Even conscience ekes in there someplace, no one knows where, shifty snake that it is. How much money, how much conscience, how much risk, pain, pleasure, effort? Why do they need me for these chances? Are they so afraid for themselves that they spend all this energy checking me out and cutting me in?

Well, they came to the right nine-toed, French-speaking, lovelorn fellow.

She hadn't touched her breakfast. When she left, I ate her croissants and her little buttered tartines, I drank her milk and coffee, I wished there were orange juice, but I was feeling better than I could remember feeling. I was in business again.

**6** I used to get to Paris now and then. When I was an
eye, a French-speaking eye, plus perhaps the fifth
or sixth best eye in San Francisco—but easily the
best French-speaking one—I used to get subcontracted
onto collection jobs, child-finding jobs, divorce jobs, little
bank errands that would take me to France and sometimes
to Geneva. Never anything complicated. If I had to remember numbers, I wrote them on my fly. Enough to keep my
French in practice and lose my slight accent indochinois.

This deal was more complicated and I'm not sure my
French was the reason.

I strolled around the knotted medieval streets of the Left
Bank, with that light and easy feeling you get after good
and irresponsible love-making, when you don't need to
tend to the lady afterward and before the loneliness sets in
again. Luci gives that feeling; the streets of Paris have been
giving that feeling for centuries. Most of the plane trees
were gone from the Boul Mich and the boulevard St.-Ger-
main. The cobblestones had been tarred over. The stench
of non-emission-controlled traffic was worse than Burbank.
The noise level was terrible. The bread has had the wheat
germ removed and they use industrial yeast for fast baking

and maybe sodium propanate to retard aging and the baguette I bought got thrown at a clochard in the Place Maubert. How dare they ruin the bread. The girls, even the young ones, had green skin and sunken eyes. They were tearing down the old buildings and building investment condos right here in the center of that best garden of the world. Nothing was as good as it used to be. I was happier than I could remember.

Something to do at last! Good-bye war in the head every morning. I was picking my own dangers again.

I took a deep breath of darling Paris pollution and headed toward the rue de l'Hôtel Colbert and the hotel I needed. On the little streets from which traffic was banned, the air sweetened considerably. No difference.

I was thinking about being an enforcer just by my mere presence.

I was thinking about how people get in trouble just from needing money, occupation, something to get in trouble about.

"Attention!" said a giggling voice, and I jumped. "Bon!"

I was reeling against a plane tree (the police and planners have left a few), stepping in crusts of dog caca, and fighting for the light of day after a blow on the side of the head from what felt like a Chicago surplus blackjack. It might have bent my skull toward permanent epilepsy if I didn't have one of those happy, skippy, American boy walks—and that "Attention!" which tended to alert me— and it just skimmed on past the jet-lag debris, ripping at my ear, a little blood soon, and I caught sight of a short, fat, waddling black priest in purple robes and a briefcase but I wasn't even sure if he was the one.

I looked around me.

My ear was bleeding. My head ached. I felt fine and decided to go ask Mahmoud at the Hôtel des Trois Portes if he had anything for a nearly mortal crush on the head.

The man at the desk gazed curiously past my head. I suppose he was admiring the handkerchief pressed to my ear. Yes, Monsieur Mahmoud was in his room. He was expecting me. I could go up.

Mahmoud opened the door before I knocked and bowed me in with clucking noises. There was a tin-framed Kodachrome photograph on the flimsy hotel desk—a solemn black priest in purple robes of the sort that ambles on by after offering a little head wound.

"Hi," I said, "you still understand the American language?"

"You ask questions, Meester Kasdan?"

I grabbed his ear and twisted and used my fingernails. "So now we're approximately even," I said.

"I will kill you," he said.

"No, you won't."

"We could have killed you in the street, as you saw. But we chose not to."

I shrugged. "I could have pulled your ear off and mailed it to Vincent van Gogh, but I chose not to."

"What?"

"Never mind. Why you play that game?"

"To let you know we will not be cheated or betrayed."

"Nobody said you would be."

"I am strong. We are very strong."

That was funny. "I'll be the judge of that," I said. "So far, not."

"What do you need?"

"Getting slugged from behind doesn't make it for me," I said. "Understand something. You try to hurt me, I'll try to hurt you. You try to kill me, you won't last at all. Better figure another way."

"Okay okay okay."

We sat down. No special hospitality. I told him what I had figured out. He wasn't very important. Probably not

27

Luci, either. That they were still testing me. That I wanted the principals now. That I should be taken off probation. That if I was going to do a job, I wanted to begin. That Mahmoud should do his job as if I were not there, but know that I was there. Lead me correctly. And no more practical jokes.

"Okay," he said.

"I'm reminding you."

"Okay."

"So now I think I'll just relax a little and try to see something pretty in this town until your people decide what you want."

"Maybe we know," he said, "but we do not have your impatience. Perhaps it would calm you to find a girl?"

"What diseases she got?"

"None. Curiosity."

"I don't have the antidote to that. It's catching."

Mahmoud said, "You got it, meester."

So he thought I knew what he was doing and supposed to do. But Luci had not told me.

"I'll see Our Lady instead," I said.

"Notre-Dame. Nice church. They dug a parking garage in the piazza in front."

He was a peculiar mixture of linguist and nonlinguist, smart and dumb. He was fat and greasy, just as he was supposed to be, but he had neat little well-behaved baby jowls like a squirrel's on each side of his face. Well, I didn't have to like Mahmoud.

"You speak Italian?" I asked.

"Italian, French, Creole, Arabic, English a leetle, haha, and Rumanian."

*"Rumanian?"*

"You like to meet nice Rumanian girl, Meester Sid?"

"Tell her," I said, "I'll meet her near a guitar player in the plaza above the parking garage at Notre-Dame's church. Tomorrow at six."

"Tomorrow. After your siesta. All-important fact is that you not worry or suffer distress, Meester Sid."

So I walked back past the cheese shops and art galleries of the rue de Seine, the rue de Buci, thinking his word "distress." I figured they wanted both to test my stubbornness and to wear me down. They, whoever *they* were—not Luci, not Mahmoud—wanted to make sure I was foolhardy. They wanted to engage me tightly and knew me pretty well. They knew I engage differently from most. I need to get my melancholia out of gear and my dreams engaged. I need to end grief. So the cash Luci had handed me so negligently needed to be given other weight. I had this flattering idea that they chose me from the whole wide world of eyes, gun-runners, surplus smugglers, defrocked CIA men because I was uniquely tired of myself.

I'm sure they wanted me to get the idea I was special. Luci in bed was a division of that enterprise. I needed it, and I didn't even try to hide how I needed it. That's okay. I needed it for myself.

The TV cameras come out, and the police and the rioters and the riotees all get brave. The storekeeper waves his fist, too. Courage is hard to find outside now; it's hard to find inside, too.

The rule should be: If anyone is watching, it's not courage. No friends or enemies to cheer or disappoint. No lovers or children to exalt. I doubt if I have any serious friends, lovers, or ex-wife; probably not. But I am watching myself very closely. For myself I do this.

Isn't this an awful vanity? Well, maybe not. Not vanity but desperation. Not courage but rashness. Priscilla: I can't think of anything else to do from day to day.

I sat in the little café in front of my hotel and stared at the statue of Diderot, raising his finger to the ancient church. A consortium of green-skinned French models and pederasts was gathered at the next table to discuss a photo layout. And at the table to the other side of me a woman with a boy child was instructing him in the proper taking of the French tea ceremony. She was his mother, but he might have been a pageboy and she the horny mistress of a knight long gone to war. "Do it this way, chéri." "Oui, maman."

I wished to travel: dreams. I wished to destroy my deathly calm: anxiety. This road I followed was a way to happy suicide.

Mahmoud! Luci! You make me happy.

But my brain was undamaged, it seems, for it came to me just then to wonder: Why did she say Luci *Worthington* with that amused, winking emphasis?

7 A day in waiting for my Rumanian contact. Another day I didn't need to get over Luci's breakfast and Mahmoud's friend's exploration of the side of my head. Whatever game they were playing with me, they were also testing me. They were also bent on committing me to them. Okay, I had no other life, so let's go.

Mahmoud: He looked like the manager of a chain of inner-city short-order drive-ins. Not a franchise yet, but maybe a degree in business from San Jose State. He was neat all the way up and down, and smily, and greedy, and dangerous. And worst of all—not reckless.

Luci: Aside from my pleasure in her company, and her fuzz all over, and her prettiness, and that sweet picklish smell, she was in the business of trouble for me, whatever good she also did. I seemed to be in the business of finding cool woman trouble.

Mahmoud: squirrel jowls and fat lips. He may have been smart; he may have been an idiot savant with a taste for languages and money. I suspect he took better care of his head than of his body. These days he was wearing a black suit of some North African version of plastic doubleknit—sheep's wool, maybe. He lumbered full of grace. He had no afterthoughts.

In fact, they both seemed to lack afterthought. I suppose that's why Luci seemed so strange to me: no conscience. But it's also how I knew that whatever they had in mind, it would surely distract me from my time filled with too many sleepless mornings and dreams of grief. I needed to get rid of afterthoughts. Oh, but good to have broodings for breakfast when you are me.

Which I do. Me: About to be middle-aged, maybe yesterday. I got through the days, but it was the nights when the girl I once loved, once married, who left me a year or two ago, when I was a mere kid and should get over it quickly, came back to keep me from sleep. No, she let me doze, but then I awakened with a start: She's smoke in my head! and I'm still funking! So I was an ambulatory target for anything from Luci Worthington or Mahmoud that can distract such a boy.

I sat at the Café de Notre-Dame and watched the tourists filling out their gargoyle postcards.

If they were testing me, patience was a thing they would test.

But I knew their remarks were not wasted. She had said her name was Luci Worthington. He had said Rumanian, he spoke Rumanian, he pulled that peculiar one on me.

Okay, thinking is not impatience. I turned Mahmoud and Luci—who were surely only representatives—into their natural question. They perform an interesting traffic in what?

Pharmaceuticals?

Arms?

Hot money?

Plutonium?

I think I'd prefer hot money best, it's so portable, but no one gave me a choice in the matter. I'm sure to be a mule, lugging something from here to there. But so far, Mahmoud looks like the mule and I'm only the watchdog. But that's only a guess.

Another Perrier might relieve the impatience in my liver. The Swedish postcard people at the next table had gone and they were replaced by Austrian lovers in ski sweaters, hugging and squeezing—both boys.

Perhaps Mahmoud's Rumanian friend will help me in more ways than the one he indicated (buy guide to Notre-Dame, pass the time). I imagined a girl from a rather late stage of Rumanian history, advanced boxy cheaply made suit, with dew on her upper lip, held there by cilia. Nothing like what I met. If she were sad, I thought, I would comfort her by taking her to bed. But if I were sad, she wouldn't do the same for me.

So I wouldn't be sad.

And what made me think my taking her to bed would be a comfort to this flashing, laughing Rumanian?

Here she comes. Stop doubting.

8 Inflation and the price of things have cut down on the Bohemians of Paris, but among the diminished foreign biders of time left, the street buskers singing in front of the cafés or in the métro, the consciousness-expanded just back from Katmandu or Scarsdale with their garage-sale heads, quite a few hang out on that pseudopark roof of the garage below the square in front of Notre-Dame. German girls are picking up black guys. Arabs are arguing and waiting for evening, blinking in the sun. Vents through the grass are voiding the carbon monoxide from below. A group was clustered about a Danish country rock guitarist, singing in American about that lonesome road, twanging away in front of the hallowed old cathedral. One of his listeners was wearing a silken frock of some flowered design, orange-colored, of oranges, powerful shapes and colors, but not so strong as the blue-black hair, the blue-black eyes, the palely glowing skin. "I am lady from Bucharest," she said.

"You speak English or French?"

"A little and un peu."

"Like our friend Mahmoud, yes?"

"Yes and no."

"Shall we get acquainted here?"

She shrugged. The fumes from the parking structure below leaked through this tourist parade ground. The Danish guitarist was driving ole Dixie down. Girls young enough to be the daughters of Joan Baez lay reverently on bedrolls around him. "You look at me kind of funny," she said.

"What I'd kind of like to know is, am I watching you or you watching me? What's your name?"

"Maybe both. Magda, of course."

"Of course. And now that we've cleared everything up, we have a coffee?"

We walked through the little park along the Left Bank side of Notre-Dame, past the monument to the Resistance, across the footbridge to the Île St.-Louis, down the rue de l'Île St.-Louis, past a dark church with cool air rushing through it and a sherbet shop with lines out on the street; and finally, on a boulevard which seemed to lead toward the Bastille, we stopped in a café. She was breathing through her mouth. That glowing upper lip had a few drops of dew on it. Some American tourists enjoy walking. "You always like this," she asked, "so quickly?"

"You always complain, Magda?"

We sat behind a glass screen on the terrace. She used both her sugars.

The waiter forgot for a moment that being a waiter in France is a distinguished profession and slammed down the glass of water I asked for. Probably thought I was a mere American capitalist tourist. Which I was; only I was here on business.

"Mahmoud," Madame Magda said, "wants to know how much trouble you will make him."

"How much he need?"

"You always answer a question with a question?"

"Have I been doing that?"

She laughed. I covered her hand. She removed her hand. "I don't hold hands," she said, "unless I make love. And I'm not sure I make love with you."

I held her hand.

"You answer my question," she said.

"Only two ways to distract me from Mahmoud," I said. "First and foremost is tell me what business he's in."

"Same business you're in, only the other end."

"What business is that?"

"Same one."

"We're getting noplace, my friend."

She smiled. "You're holding my hand. But it doesn't count if you grab and I not offer." Then she leaned forward and gazed into my eyes. "You mean—" she started to laugh "—you mean you don't *know?*"

"I know I'm getting something for watching over things. I suppose I'm safe against certain forms of questioning if I don't really know."

"You think you're safe?" she asked. "You're safe against telling, but you think you're safe against being asked?"

"What?"

"I should believe—you mean you really don't know?—ignorance needs to worry a clever person. Mister Sid, have you considered that you might look more clever than you are, if foresight is a part of cleverness?"

"Hold. Hold."

"All I am saying can be summed up in ancient and honorable Rumanian folk wisdom: Ignorance is seldom bliss. If others don't know you are ignorant, they can blame you. And as Haitian peasant says: Stupidity won't kill you, but it can make you sweat a lot."

She had a point. Several points. I began to see her point. Two or three of them. The fact is, despite my too busy dream life, I manage to require distraction, to get into trouble. And now, if I took her back to wherever she lived, would she ask me for answers I couldn't give? Or would there be someone else to ask and make me sweat?

"So let us go to your hotel," she said.

I had been thinking aloud; she hadn't read my mind. As distraction goes, it was clear enough. To the cab driver I said, "Hôtel Madison." To the cab driver she said, "Hôtel des Trois Portes," and then gave him instructions about how to get there. Too much traffic. We got off at the Place St.-André-des-Arts and walked. On the rue Xavier-Privas there was an Arab shouting at another, "Don't push me!" and the other one saying, "You pushed me!" and the first one saying, "I don't like to be pushed!" and the first one saying ... We didn't stay for the fight. A few steps away, in the doorway of the Crêmerie Concorde, two cops with those leaded capes were watching, racist smiles under their little mustaches.

Now that she could tell Mahmoud I didn't know what I was watching for, I saw no reason to be afraid of Mahmoud. I felt pretty cheerful. "Magda Worthington?" I said. She just smiled and shook her head and wiped the dew from her upper lip. It was like a paid vacation and I would just ride with the flow, a true California mind.

There was no elevator at the Hôtel des Trois Portes. We went to Room 27, three floors up. I followed her little behind snuggled among the orange silk flowers. Yummy. My missing big toe had begun to ache, but I didn't mind. She knocked twice and the door opened and a black priest swung at me. "What are you doing here?" he yelled as I ducked and made ready for violence.

"She brought me."

"Right off he said he didn't know what Mahmoud was carrying," said Magda.

The priest sank to the bed with his head in his hands. "Oh, Christ, you are a waste of time."

"You have to give me the information. You have to tell me what not to tell. You have to sketch out the area of my ignorance. You have to make me informed in addition to so-called quick—"

"Which I'm not so sure you are," he said.

That made two of them within the hour with such an opinion.

"You could start by telling me your name," I said.

"Father Brice," he said, pronouncing it Brees. "I'm Haitian, but I trained in an American seminary. I took orders with Americans."

"Lots of people do," I said.

"Now you know everything, dummy."

"Now you better tell more, father. For example, that samurai trick in the street. If you're testing my reflexes, why not just ask me to walk a white line?"

He smiled. "This was so much better, my son. You moved spritely for a man our age."

My self-respect did not depend on his approval. "I can only go so far on my own," I said. "I thought Magda was Mahmoud's and maybe a little bit mine, but now I find she's yours. And where's Miss Worthington?"

He started at the name. "Okay. Okay. Okay. Sit down, please."

I was already doing so.

"Magda, leave the room." So there were things she didn't know either. "Sid, I'll explain. Please, my dear."

Miss Bucharest departed. Brice hung a towel on the doorknob to block the keyhole. This seemed a rather primitive procedure for the scientific struggle against electronic or other bugging, but to each his own. This branch of the Church Episcopal had its own cute ways. He said he would have to tell me, but I should understand it might cost me dear. Money? No, life expectancy.

I considered the point. What was it worth? "Okay, tell me," I said.

"Models," he said.

"*What?* Models of what?"

"The French franc is strong," he said. I already knew this. And the American dollar and the British pound are weak; this month, anyway. "We have a little deal in models for France, Germany, the Arab emirates." He was amused at my lack of comprehension. I was less amused at his failure of communication. "How to explain to a person like you who is not driven by his passions? Rather made sluggish by them—a sin, my son."

"Just say it," I said. "Specify. Is it the item or just the model? Is it mass shipment or detail? Is it—"

"Very well, by the detail," he said. "I have one in the next room. It's for Mahmoud and I want to make sure I get the money before I deliver."

"Let's go into the next room."

He nodded and we stood up together.

In Room 28 of the Hôtel des Trois Portes there was a young man sitting on the bed in a white shirt and white pants, no shoes, reading a French comic book. He was moving his lips as he read. He finished the page, looked up at me, smiled, and made a kissing noise with his lips. He was black, with one of those perfect, healthy, round African heads, covered with very tight curls. His skin gleamed. His eyes gleamed. He made those kissing noises in my direction.

"Fais gentil," said Father Brice.

The boy stopped the noises.

"What is this?" I asked.

"He's Haitian."

"I get a whiff of slave trade."

"Well, he's not chained or something on that order. But you get a correct whiff."

"So what is this?"

"You are familiar, of course, with the rapidly evolving temper of the times and how everyone is so honest about his desires. And how there are tired businessmen in Hamburg, in Paris, in New York, in Beirut, very much in the Arab emirates, not in Libya, however, and all they ask is a modicum of relaxation from the cares of the day, money, wives, children—"

"Yeah, I know all that."

"Especially relief from their wives. Well, I had a colleague bought blood from Haiti, because there's a worldwide shortage of plasma, but I thought to myself: Heck, that's immoral. Starving people shouldn't be persuaded to sell their blood. But then I had this other idea, me with my American partners did, we thought there are the boys would like a good international education—"

"Say on."

"I shall if you will not keep interrupting me."

I bit my lip. The boy was deep into his educational comic book. How you say Superman in French is Surhomme. He could have been eighteen, I suppose; old enough to vote; old enough to service a tired oil sheik. Father Brice was still explaining. He didn't kidnap these kids. He paid their parents. He got their consent. Of course, they might not understand some things about worldwide travel, but they knew what they would have to do once they got there. It was in the tradition. Many of them would come home later, cash in a few presents they had received or walked off with, marry the village sweetheart, have kids, nothing lost. In fact, a lot gained. It was their only chance to get some good shirts, good cologne, good table habits.

"Shit," I said. "What has all this other jokery been about?"

Father Brice wanted their position about men understood. There is a delicacy in trade. The boys were given spending money and entertainment, too. They felt it important to get me interested with the suggestions my own imagination would provide about hot funds, narcotics, fissionable material. This was a very much older business. They had discovered it was a difficult time in my life. I suited them; yet they were not sure. "We had to get you involved," he said. "We want you to give up your other sources of income—"

"I don't have any."

"We know that. Of entertainment, then."

"Even less."

"Okay. You are here. Now you understand. Are you ready?"

"Shit," I said.

"I suppose you want to know more about what you will do." An assumption. "Well, there are problems. We have to escort the trade. It can't be packed and shipped alone. We need to make sure they don't get lost or run away. You speak French, you can keep them from growing melancholique with the homesickness. You are polite. You make the transfer introductions, let's say in Hamburg, and—"

"I don't speak German."

"Never mind. English or French will do." He waited to see if I wished to express myself further. I didn't. "Sometimes there is tact involved. You are not very tactful sometimes, but you can be if you wish to be. You must remember we are dealing in love. And yet we must deal expeditiously, sometimes even rapidly. Love should not be like this, but alas, my son, in this world here below, sometimes it is. Sometimes we send the client a photograph of a lad and then there's a problem, we turn up with a different lad. You have to explain. You have to show how it is a good lad anyway."

I suddenly remembered they hadn't given me a round-trip ticket to San Francisco. What was I thinking of? When I still had my license, I would never have taken a job without a roundtrip ticket.

Did I want to be, well, not a white slaver? A black slaver?

"I realize you knew very little or nothing about the business. We have been organized for export only a short while. Perhaps you require time to think further, but consider this lad, he is surely contented, not drugged, quite alert." He flicked his elbow and the boy looked up. "You see? He is doing what comes natural to young lads—"

"Reading a comic book?"

"Blagueur," said Father Brice. "Only thing, we do not wish him to get lost en route. So you are more a cowboy at roundup time than a black slaver, my son. And you are a guide. You are a calming agency. You are an introducer. Nothing like chains or a leash, but you must move the lads on and off airplanes, through customs, check the visas, note the time changes, then you make the contact in Abu Dhabi or Frankfurt or wherever it might need be—"

His language was slipping. It was as if he had a limited tank of correct American and he was running on empty. He was nervous. I doubted he was really in charge. And I'd lost a woman on my own, in charge of my own losing, so what good was I for corralling others? But I wasn't sure this meant I should go into the business of finding boys for men who couldn't find them themselves.

Father Brice droned on.

What the devil did Luci have to do with this?

Well, I'd abolished morality in California, like so many others, as a way of staying young. I was making it from boyhood clear into middle age without ever taking on the duties of a man, whatever they were. And I was broke. And I was stuck. And I was curious. So I might want to ride with this, too, until it didn't feel good anymore.

"You do not like the business?" Father Brice asked. "You keep saying shit and I am growing weary of it."

"Yes, sir. I'll do it," I said.

The boy looked up at me with a brilliant, welcoming smile. He didn't need to understand English. He knew something was being settled and it was about him. His eyes sparkled with anticipation. If he made that goddamn kissing noise at me one more time I'd flatten his lip a little with my fist.

But I knew I wouldn't. I wasn't being tough. I was submitting again.

**9** In another life, perhaps I was a pirate slaver with a whip and high boots and a pigskin patch over my eye. But in nonkarmic real life I'm just a sandy fellow in a sandy summer suit of mixed cotton and Dacron and a nice but not too nice Cable Car Clothiers tie. There was no chain around the neck of the slave. I would jerk on the chain if this pretty Haitian boy made his kissy-kissy sound at me again. If I had him tied with a chain, and I didn't.

Father Brice must have given him a heavy trank. He sat slumped sideways in his seat on the France-Inter flight from Le Bourget to Frankfurt. He snapped out of his nod when the stewardess—an Air France reject, I guessed, for the crime of pug nostrils—came by with coffee and sandwiches. He chewed thoughtfully with his eyes half-shut. I wanted to ask him if he was thinking, What's a nice Haitian boy like me doing in a job like this?

Or maybe he was like an American kid on the road to Big Sur, just letting matters roll on. Had anyone described his duties in detail? Was he expected simply to know? Was there a job specification report? Were the preferences of the Frankfurt purchaser laid out for his approval? He was rubbing his hands. Not anticipation. The dryness of airplane travel and the changed climate. Young fellow like him doesn't prefer very much to have dry hands.

I believed that this transport to Frankfurt was a shakedown cruise for something else. That the good father was training me, preparing me, testing me for a mission to the production facilities in Haiti. That I wanted to do this right if I wanted to do it at all. One of my problems is carrying through what I start. (My wife had to leave *me;* I wasn't going to end it.) I believed Luci and Mahmoud and the good Father Brice were all stages on life's way that someone else had planned for me. Magda was only one small step for mankind. I might be a step on someone else's way.

And yet there could still be problems with the man in Frankfurt, whom I imagined to be a good burgher with wife and seven kids, thick, rich, pork-nourished, and creepy. He had to be different in some ways, although he too was looking to interrupt the steady march of the days.

The Frankfurt Airport is one of those anonymous postwar glass-and-concrete and moving belts and aluminum and international, multinational, outerspace jobs. It could be Milan. It could be Kansas City. If they were speaking German, this must be Germany. They were speaking German.

I wondered what customs would think. I wasn't exactly smuggling in this Haitian kid, but what if they didn't like looking at the middle-aged nervous sandy American and the black Haitian lad and thus decided to strip me to look up some orifices, down different ones, to see if I was stashing even odder goods on my person? I didn't enjoy this wait. I'd had some difficulties with grass already that got my credentials cancelled. I'd prefer to be half of a pair of young lovers, back from a weekend near the Eiffel Tower. But when the Gestapo customs veteran glanced at my passport, he flipped up the GeKlosed sign on his window, leav-

ing other travelers stranded in the line, and crooked his polite little pinkie at me, and gave me a lesson in being important. He led me around to the black and gold VIP door.

It wasn't I who was important, of course. It was Herr
Doktor Professor Industrialist Pederastische who waited
for us with a rosebud pinned to his lapel. He carried another in purplishly oiled paper. He was waiting standing
up. He had shaved within the last hour. He was trying not
to show the smile of a dream come true at last. He handed
the rose to Lucky Pierre, not his real name, my charge.
"Merci, m'sieu," said the lad, staring closely as if he might
have to eat it. Careful, lad; the rose has thorns.

"How do you do?" I asked, unasked. "Do I just turn
around and go back now? Is there an airport hotel where I
can freshen up a little before I leave?"

"O sir, no sir," said the lover. "You are my guest for the
day and night, with no cost to you at all, of course not, sir."
He glanced at Pierre.

"He doesn't look nervous, but underneath it all, he probably is," I said.

"Of course, of course, so natural, you will reassure him."

"Since we're old friends," I said.

"I must show you Frankfurt. My factory. My warehouse. My family home."

"That about does it," I said.

He didn't mind what I said. He may not even have heard
it. He was an impacted structure of meat which looked as if
it had once been larger, had been pressed down by experi-
ence. His face folded upon face; his nose extruded the slack.
If Porky were mostly muscles instead of fat, this would be
a piggy herr fellow. I tried to dislike him, but it didn't work
out. He was simply there. "The pig is the most intelligent
animal; it never looks at the sky."—Proverb. I was there
and he was there and Pierre was in for it. My Frankfurt client wanted me along for awhile, perhaps to chaperone. Did

he fear rude advances from Pierre? Did he want a witness for boyish events? He wanted their relationship to grow. Pierre was his sky for looking at. He wanted to Get to Know Him. I was needed to interpret, perhaps for Herr Schwartz, which means black. Did this overweight shy porker with a collarbone covered with warts love black boys because they were a translation of himself, whom he loved dearly?

He gazed at Pierre with the lovelook of yearning in his eye. It was the look in my mirror in the morning in Poorman's Cottage when I awoke from that dream, again and again, of Priscilla Kasdan, the wife I once thought joined to me in San Francisco.

Was I a translation of this emeritus Nazi in Frankfurt?

All I could observe for sure was about his little wart and avoirdupois condition. The rest—clever, crazy, Nazi nostalgia, plus well-to-do—might ooze out in due course. Pierre took the rose in one hand, the hand of Herr Schwartz in the other. I carried the bags. Herr Schwartz disengaged his paw and affixed the rose to Pierre's lapel with a rose-headed pin he carried for this purpose.

We were waved through customs without question. A smart salute with boot noises from a customs colonel, a chieftain raised far beyond slitting open corsets and gouging out cork heels. If I had owned one of those at the Tijuana border, my life might be easier.

Herr Schwartz was a big man on campus.

I toted the small straw bag. A porter carried the rest of Pierre's earthly belongings in a not very big straw bag. The two of them, plus porter, trotted ahead, silently getting to know each other. I trotted behind, trying to get to know me. A churchly echo filled this part of the terminal until we got to the long black Mercedes in which we would drive someplace.

A Turkish chauffeur bowed, opened the door, touched the brim of his cap. Herr Schwartz and Pierre cuddled without actually necking on the leather-smelling seats. I perched on a jump seat. Between us, a folding table had been extended, on which a small tummy TV sat. It was not lit. There were copies of the *International Herald-Tribune*, *The Wall Street Journal*, and something which I seem to recall as the *Conservatischezeitungeshaftjournal*, but it probably had a shorter name. Another newspaper. They weren't being read, either.

"Fresh up?" asked Herr Schwartz.

Thinking a bath and a nap, I said, "Yes."

"Very well, then we go to my factory for tour."

Ah. A real listener.

He smiled. Lots of patriotically reclaimed tooth gold. "Iss showers at factory."

The parking lot where Herr Schwartz manufactured plastic kitchen stuff for 89¢ shops all over the world, deboners, omelet flippers, ice-cube shapers, cute colored mice with magnetized backs, was filled with VW's, but had a small section reserved for the fleet of Mercedes. Within the small section there was a smaller section reserved for one long black automobile. Here we berthed. Here we disembarked. "Ah," said Herr Schwartz, speaking for everyone. He patted Pierre's hand. Pierre had the sulky, smiling look of a brave kid in total confusion.

In a white room we received coffee on silver service. A white-coated young man—Spanish, I'd guess—brought the coffee. A Yugoslavian young man (perhaps) carried the cookies. What seemed to be a Corsican or a Sicilian boy cleaned up after our chat. What we have here is a United Nations of laddies.

He had forgotten about the showers, but as far as I was concerned, this was just as well. I wasn't ready for a Hitler Youth towel boy.

"You speak Cherman?" Herr Industrialische asked Alois Portrait-de-Dieu (Pierre's real name).

"No," I answered for him.

47

Herr Schwartz turned his back on me and repeated: "You speak German!" This was an order which Alois could not obey despite the best will in the world.

"Tu parles français?"

"Petit-petit, m'sieu."

Herr Schwartz turned a face toward me which contradicted his wide behind, his stubby thighs, his heft and age; it was a lyrical sweet gasp of delight and love. They could communicate! The boy's French was really Creole, a fusion of French and African dialects, and the industrialist's was Army of Occupation Pidgin. He was no silken gigolo. They would get along somehow. What further need of me? I asked myself.

"I have no further need of you," said the German.

The two were beginning to look yearningly at each other. The boy was smiling and blowing on his coffee to cool it, making little swirls of steam which immediately dissipated, like most true love. So I should go while everything was still nice. They needed each other and did not need me.

"Au revoir," I started to say and finished saying, as the Turkish chauffeur opened the door (what button summoned him?).

The room seemed to spin on its axis. The Haitian boy's face crumpled. His eyelids fluttered wildly. He clung to me, weeping. He was homesick. I was his daddy. This was summer camp. Whom was I leaving him with? What was happening to him?

"Tais-toi!" screamed the German. Shut Up is a phrase which we understand even if we don't understand it. And in this shriek lay command and threat. The boy subsided, his chest throbbing with hiccups. I left.

If I hadn't suspected it already, mixing money and love was difficult in all its aspects. Alois, this lucky Pierre, this

48

nonwar bride, had been in my charge for only a short time. I had delivered him. Now I delivered myself elsewhere.

The Turkish chauffeur was trying to speak English and succeeding as we drove toward the airport. Herr Schwartz wished to make sure I got there promptly. He was courteous. He supplied an escort. The escort was saying in his softly guttural boy's voice, "Sir? Throw up."

"Pardon?"

"Sir. Throw up."

"Pardon."

He slowed down at the corner. I caught a glimpse of my gray and yellow face in the mirror. I jumped out and stuck my finger down my throat and did my best, gagging and knocking against the fender of the Mercedes. The chauffeur waited a bit anxiously. He had a cloth ready in case I stained the finish. He would wipe it away. The acid of vomit, especially the acid of poison in vomit, tends to mar the fine finish. I leaned, retching, against the car.

"You will be all right, sir. Very slow to act. He want you out of the country first."

"Thank you very much."

"Not necessary to let him know I—"

"Right. You and I have our little secret. Thank you."

He tipped his hat with Turkish courtesy. He delivered me to the airport, brooding on why he did this good deed. Maybe he thought I was Armenian and the honor of Turkey called for a gesture. I thanked him very much. I was lonely for Luci. I was a little less lonely for Miss Bucharest. I was somewhat sickened by the intentions of others. I had a glimpse—or rather, a taste—of why the Holy Family needed me to do this job. They were dealing in a perishable commodity and unstable clients. A jealous or angry or worried man could seek to dissolve the links between his cocoa boy and the Worthingtons. Harm could come someone's way: mine. They needed a disposable but not overly stupid mule: me. The intentions of others are often sickly.

I was also sickened by unsureness about my own intentions. Perhaps ending the bad dreams in Poorman's Cottage is not enough reason to enter a whole career of bad dreams. I told myself again: But the boys are better off here or anywhere than in Haiti, where the children's bellies are again distended with kwashiokor; they know what they're doing; they'll go back after awhile to their village sweethearts with some European shirts and shaving lotion and some American dollars; even their parents are happy.

And what I'm doing now is better than what I was doing a month ago in Poorman's Cottage. Moping is a form of slavery, too. Sid Kasdan, the nine-toed moper. I don't see any chains on anyone's legs. I don't see any whipmarks, do I?

I tried to like what I was doing while I went about discovering what it was.

I suppose this attempt to poison Sid Kasdan, rational courier, brought me back to survival concerns—love and loss. Those are negative memories. The positive one is memory of the appetites I might feel once again in the future.

**10** Landing slightly queasy but okay at Le Bourget Airport near Paris, I made a deal with the first North African cab driver I found. I hurried to the address on the rue Xavier-Privas. Father Brice and Luci were waiting. I grabbed the good father by the collar of his Pierre Cardin caftan: "What the fuck he try to poison me?"

"How'd it go?" Brice asked calmly.

"Why the fuck he try to poison me?" I was correcting my grammar.

"He wouldn't do that."

"Son of a bitch Nazi faggot tried to poison me!"

"Are you not a Jewish person?"

"Shut up with the jokes! He tried to poison me!"

Luci said, "You don't even say hello and it's been so long, Sid."

Brice shrugged. "You look okay to me, a little green at the edges."

"I was lucky. Hello. I could have been dead."

"But you're not," Luci said sweetly, "we can witness to that."

"I am pleased, also," Brice said. "But let me now answer your question. First: I have no reason on earth or in heaven to wish you anything but good health and good digestion, my friend. What the client did or did not do—you make him angry somehow, you irritate him? No? Okay. One: He is afraid of blackmail. Two: He desires to cut back on the boy's escape routes. Three: He thinks you might blackmail him. That's one again. Personally, I congratulate you for not dying, and in general, you must realize this, we are reimbursing you to accept some degree of risk."

I stared and waited for him to make me feel better. I wasn't going to look at Luci. I didn't want that kind of feeling better from her now.

"Here," said Brice. He handed me an envelope. I unfolded it. There was a stack of hundred-dollar bills inside. I didn't count them. "No deductions for social security or taxes. You find a way to handle that problem yourself. This contest is void wherever state or local regulations prohibit." He peered into my face to try to detect the signs of greed. There may have been some. I felt like sitting on a bed in a hotel room and counting.

I said: "This is my second envelope. We never discussed terms."

"Because we are so generous," said Brice, "and besides, you are not engageable by money."

"I'm an idealist," I said. "I'm just doing this instead of—"

Brice interrupted me. "Now receive a word. There are crazy persons everywhere in this business. They are unpredictable. Even we are unpredictable. You understand by this time. But you will be paid well. Besides money, which I will offer you from time to time, I can give you advice: Rediscover your agility and try to avoid poisoners, shooters, dumpers, crazies whom you can't predict. Is that clear?"

I nodded because it would be foolish to say yes. The nod said I understood, while a yes would have been bragging.

I would do my best not to get poisoned by crazies whom I did not predict. Also not to get garroted, shot, run over by trucks (in England, lorries), stabbed, or infected with hepatitis. And eventually I would either launder or squander my money. I had my work cut out for me, exactly what is required in order to forget a faithless wife. Perhaps every man deserted by a modern woman—one who must go out in the world to seek her freedom, her prince, her space— needs to find a new occupation, such as black slavery. Thank you, modern persons of all the continents. You too have the right to happiness. So do I. I was in receipt of Father Brice's words.

The residual effects of Herr Schwartz's permanent analgesic had expanded my consciousness a bit. It occurred to me that Brice and Mahmoud did not communicate a good sense of my employer, nor did Luci Worthington. But the stack of bills did. Hundred-dollar notes in such quantity—

"By the way, son, there are thirty of them," Brice said. —give a fellow a chance to enjoy some of the things that money can buy, especially if this is only a healthy start.

"That's only a start," Brice said. "In a sense, we are testing. You will do better. I should tell you, though, that the first twenty are genuine."

I opened the envelope and flipped through the stack. The first twenty were wrinkled, dirty, and authentic after their various sea voyages. The last ten bore a cross-eyed American hero, identical numbers, and a sickly pale green tint. It didn't smudge, but it didn't convince, either. Without a word I thrust them back at the good father.

He shrugged. "That was a kind of bonus. Okay, if you choose not. Surely we owe you no more."

"That's a business I want no part of."

"Very well. Personally, it puts more money in circulation, increases the traffic of money and goods. I have never understood the objections to a little stimulation of the economy, since international trade is my chosen field of endeavor. Very well if you are frightened or scared, however."

"No. Both."

"Okay. It will not come up again. There is the pity of it. You will never be really wealthy."

"I accept that."

"Just the same as surely no German client will try to poison you again."

"I welcome that, too."

Luci put a coin into an imaginary machine and her arm with its long hand and curled fingers became a crane and swung around and she cranked it down and it plucked the ten pale green cross-eyed Federal Reserves out of Father Brice's hands. "She likes them," he said. (She smiled.) "She has a way with people." (She sucked in her cheeks. She looked winsome.) "She buys, say, black market francs from Corsicans with these. It is very beautiful to watch her."

"I could get hurt," Luci remarked happily.

"You get killed for this sort of thing," I said.

"I could get hurt."

"But she smiles," said Brice, "and they don't look too closely, and so far she accomplishes nothing along the line of hurt or killed. Of course, she is wearing out cities. Where will you change these?"

Luci smiled. "Not Paris. Not Geneva. Not Marseilles. Not Milan. East Berlin, maybe. Moscow, maybe. I haven't worn out so many cities, father."

"It's a whole side of you I didn't know," I said.

Sweetly she sighed. "You poor boys. If one like you, not a pig, a really nice boy, you think because you look deep into my eyes, you are supposed to know me through and through."

"I didn't see that they're a little crossed inside."

54

"You say?"

"Inside. And look at this Founding Father here—really crossed eyes. You too, Luci, only it's not visible."

"That's the only kind of crossed eyes I want, Al—" was that my name now? "—only I think we should all do our best to put more money in circulation, give jobs to our minority peoples, increase the traffic of money and goods." Brice was nodding as she spoke. He approved of her echo. A man like Brice always knows when people are saying the right things: when they say exactly what he has just said. Luci chucked him under the chin. Good boy.

"Okay, let's get matters clear and straight," I said. "I'll put up with some surprises, but I don't want them to be tricks on me. Just plain surprise will do. I'll do this job we talked about. The boys are not drugged. They have been consulted. They're willing. It's a job. I'll do them for you. I'll transport. But no counterfeit, no narcotics, no arms, no illegal nothing, you hear? Not even tax-free cigarettes for the smoking masses."

"I hear, I hear," Father Brice said. "Where are the enterprising international entrepreneurs of yesteryear?"

"No plans for atomic weapons. No maps of installations. I'm not even sure about unwilling women. I want you to be straight with me, Brice. Level with me, Luci."

They looked bewildered at each other. This was a puzzle and a dilemma. Luci spoke first: "I'm not sure that's possible, Sid. I even call you Al sometimes."

"Call me anyone you like."

"Sometimes we trank the boys down a little for the rigors of jet travel, Sid."

"Okay. I've done that to myself a few times, too. So long as you tell me and you're straight. Okay? Is that it?"

Father Brice seemed deeply distressed. "Please, my friend. Ask not what a person cannot give. Please."

Luci and Brice fell silent. I waited. Gradually she took

her ease, took my hand, lay another hand on the back of my neck, gazed into my eyes, and said: "Look back. You seem kind of distrait. It was a hard trip. That ugly pharmaceutical and everything. I understand, Sid. You need some rest. It isn't jet lag this time, but it's a kind of nervous, isn't it? Okay. Poor boy. Listen: Wanna poke around really deep in my immortal soul and fuck?"

# 11

I slept less well than if I had accepted Luci's kind offer. Even though this promise might very well not be repeated, I could not. I have some heart and the heart I have hates heartlessness. Oh, she was friendly. But there was a core of cross-eyed counterfeit in the offer.

A Quaalude calmed me instead. There's a sincere and open companion for sleep.

The next morning Father Brice bustled in with Luci to wake me (tray of coffee for three, pitcher of hot milk, croissants, jams, butters, that delicious blood-wrecking French breakfast). Luci did not resemble a rejected woman. Her heart lay unbroken in her neat and skimpy chest. She looked like a business lady—horn-rimmed glasses, librarian's bun of hair, plans.

"You're okay," Brice said.

"We're really sorry about the pharmaceuticals."

"That's all right," I said modestly, "about the poison. Could happen to anyone, anytime. Don't mean to bother you with mere details."

"Since you're ready, we are sending you straight off to World Headquarters. We trust you, Sid."

"Beverly Hills? The East Sixties? You'll have to tell me

where to go, since you can't shoot me there in a missile warhead. Could it be Chicago?"

"No, no, no, the consumer is not the problem. Supply is the most essential element of sales in this case. We need reliable, high-quality product. We want you to go to Port-au-Prince and now we'll have to explain what your job is." Brice sat down on the edge of the bed. I tipped coffee with a film of hot milk into my mouth as he lectured me about keeping up standards, finding clean boys, nice, friendly, free of chronic diseases, reasonably cooperative, no thieves as much as possible. "Sometimes a kid has a chance to be set up for life and he steals a shirt to give to some goof he meets on the street. Soap even. We had a boy stole a jar of pretty I. Magnin soaplets—bubble bath! No-brain piggy!"

"We've learned dumb kids don't work out," Luci said.

"They need a minimum IQ. They have to . . ."

Luci cut straight to the complications of international export. "It's not the boys' fault. It's our boy-farmers we deal with in Haiti. They are alert fellows, men of the world like you, all like that, but they don't really know sophisticated European and American tastes and our fetish for no diseases, no thieves, soft lips. Oh, they try to understand it pretty good, but they confuse the masochism normal to our clients with a willingness to get ripped off. It ain't necessarily so."

"Um. I feel I'm learning. I appreciate all this background material," I said.

Luci touched my hand. "First we had to be sure of you. Now we feel intelligence and understanding and a full breadth of knowledge can only help you and us both."

"I appreciate this trust," I said with dignity.

"We appreciate your appreciation," said Luci.

This was a veritable love feast. How nice to get laid, poisoned, and distracted at the hands of such thoughtful folks.

"We . . . I want you to look over the crop in Port-au-

Prince," said Brice. "I want you to make it clear. I want you to take hold as a field inspector plus transportation specialist. I want you to examine boys. Nice solid thighs and arms. A sparkle. Get them a decent suit for traveling in. Just let the local farmers know what kind of crop we need, we require, and inspect the harvest. Some solid numbers, Sid. We have good people running things in Haiti, but the international linkage requires firming up."

"You'll love Port-au-Prince," Luci said. "You may even meet some old friends."

"I don't know how good I am at firming things up."

"Good enough, I'm sure," said Luci.

"A shot of gamma globulin would be a sensible idea if you're susceptible to viruses," Brice said. "Try to avoid hepatitis, amoebiasis, intestinal parasites in general. Otherwise it's an exciting place. Paintings, music, voodoo, native crabs and lobsters, a cuisine you will adore, and a really interesting and unique form of government."

"What's that?"

"Insane tyranny and chaos. Inefficient corrupt brutality. Murder for small ransom or grudge. One of my friends was obliged to drink his lover's urine. Of course, they were irked with him. Haiti may be the loveliest nightmare you ever experienced, and I presume you have had some."

"Mostly personal," I said. "Usually not political or social ones."

"Good. Broaden your horizons," said Father Brice. "As a Haitian myself—I suppose you remember that—I have a patriotic hope that you will appreciate my native land and her folklore."

And Luci, bless her, gazed sweetly upon me, as if I could use a little horizon-broadening. No counterfeit Federal Reserve notes, no sex with her last night. I was teetering on the edge of disappointing the young woman, but also I was moving ahead in business.

59

**12** Haiti from the air is a volcanic heap of green and stone, splattered into the Caribbean near Cuba, near Europe, near Africa, near madness. From there to here is a lot of jet lag—from that dusty damp old world to this groaning, clacking, barking new one. Peasant boys fall to their deaths from a cornfield in this vertical, vertigo place. The steepness and misery seem to keep everybody laughing.

A merengue band greeted my disgorging Pan Am flight to Dr. François Duvalier International Airport, the ragged oldsters playing their tunes one more time: "Haiti Chérie," "Choucoune," and "Vive Jean-Claude Duvalier, le Jeune Leader." It gives a lift and a lilt to arrival. We lilted ourselves down into, wham! that tropical heat and humidity. I turned to take one more breath of Pan Am's air conditioning, but it was too late. The stew expelled me with a gentle touch on the elbow. *Vacarme:* That's a word imported from France. A roar out of many throats of porters, of crying babies, of lovers reunited. A few stately, portly men looked cool in their Haspel suits, Haitian officials, chilled internally by prosperity, greeted by polite, unhappy wives like the wives of the successful elsewhere. There were police in khaki uniform and Macoutes in sunglasses. The police carried sidearms and the Macoutes just carried whatever weapon was available.

Father Brice had given me a slip of paper. I was to look for someone.

"Monsieur!" cried a slim black man in a white suit. He carried a cane, plus a song in his heart. "Monsieur is perhaps a journaliste?"

No, he didn't know me.

"A man of investments seeking fields to conquer?"

"No."

"Ah. Then you are here on our business of . . ."

"No."

"Garçons?" he asked roguishly.

So I was being met after all. Why the devil didn't they tell me?

"I am Fils-Aimé, your helper in Haiti. You remember my good friend and uncle Mahmoud? He find me job as helper for you. You will please follow me and avoid nuisance of customs. You will please stay by my side and thereupon remain less tired. I have Buick Skylark for transport of you to hotel. Otherwise, sir, it is so boring in this small country—" and he tittered. "Put yourself entire in my hands and I will please regulate all, even as I am Uncle Mahmoud or Father Brice."

And quite properly, politely, decorously, he shook my hand like a good slim little Frenchman, except that he tickled my palm with his fingernail.

I found new depths of international suavity within myself. I shook his hand and it was as if I didn't notice.

"You are to descend at the Oloffson Hotel, Grand Hotel of the World," he said. "Of course, you will please most sleep and be comfortable. Elsewhere you will amuse and be practical."

"Fine."

"Anything else to desire to know?"

"I suppose I'll please find out in due course."

"So wise of you. No wonder all admire you so, Monsieur Kasdan."

We pushed past the customs people as if they were not there, a hand of young Fils-Aimé blessing my shoulder and steering me. He raised his cane to greet the chief officer. Herr Schwartz would approve. The car was parked where it said *Défense de Stationer*. It was indeed a black Buick Skylark. Fils-Aimé helped my bags in, then he helped me in. I was in capable hands and fingers. We didn't stop for a single stop sign. We drove through an antheap slum where women and chickens were nurturing their young in the street. They didn't stop for the stop signs, either. Monsieur Fils-Aimé, which was short for Son Beloved of God, also explained driving regulations in Haiti. If you hit somebody, you pay hospital expenses. If you kill him, you pay funeral expenses. Since hospital costs more than funeral, if you hit somebody, you back up and make sure he's dead.

"Thank you for doing the driving," I said.

"Human life is not worth so much," he said with a certain smugness. "To me of course it is—mine and yours. In the newspaper, when authorities list the dead, it is usually people they pick up in the street. Unknown, Male. Unknown, Female. Unknown, Child. Hahaha."

"Haha," I said politely.

"And here you are, sir," he said, "to find a few Unknown, Warm, Boy. This section of the capital is called La Saline. Only way improves is to destroy."

I tried to enjoy the tropical scenery. Palm, bamboo, rubble houses of packing crates and banana leaves. Then we climbed in lower gear through a section of thick-walled stone colonial buildings with cast-iron doorways and precarious ironwork balconies. We crossed the Place des Héros. Fils-Aimé showed me the statue of Bolivar, rejected in Colombia and sold to a defunct president of Haiti to serve as the statue of the Emperor Dessalines. "We call it the Placc dcs Zéros," he said. "You may please smile if you like."

Up a slope, it grew perceptibly cooler. The mountains in the afternoon were turning purple around the immense swarm of the city. Fewer candidates for suicide were crossing the street in front of us. A child dashed to the car window with a bunch of flowers, crying, "Gimme fi cents!" and seized the rearview mirror and was jerked off his feet as the Buick accelerated.

"Careful!" I said.

"Gimme fi cents used to mean five cents," said Fils-Aimé. "Now it just means money."

The hotel creaked on its termites' backs. It was a pellmell wooden castle, a bit musty to the nose, but with windmill ceiling fans lazily turning in the bar as I passed through. I might be happy here if I could be happy anyplace. Tourists needing something to do, someone to talk to, looked me up and down with friendly nods. I'm sure that was at least a duchess over there with the freckled bosom and the sprigs of mint between her teeth; it wasn't a rabbit. Two gets you five its breath was pure. Did I want to be happy and have a rum-soda?

Instead of happiness, business was on my mind. A meeting with our manufacturers tonight. I should prepare for agility. I'd skip the drink in favor of some dreamless tropical naptime.

Fils-Aimé came to get me after the nap I couldn't nap. I had the dreams without the sleep. I stretched my bones in the silence anyway (the silence filled with dog yaps and chicken cackles). "Very good, very good," he said while I splashed some cold water on my face. "Do not drink, please. Very good."

We drove down into the evening heat and dust. It was an oven in which civilization had been cooked until it pulverized. The streets were almost as piled with people at night as during the day. Near La Saline they lived in the streets. Kids were marching back and forth under the lampposts, chattering in a singsong, memorizing pages. There was no electricity in their houses. They were studying the verses of Racine and Corneille. "Haitian pipple adore poets of our native France," Fils-Aimé said, pounding the steering wheel with voiceless hilarity.

The boulevard Harry-Truman curved along the waterline, and then became a narrow road, and we were heading past sugar cane refineries, softball factories, and toy assembly compounds toward Bizoton. Bizoton, I repeated. I wanted to know where I was. It was a neighborhood of bars with American names, what we sometimes call massage parlors on the coasts of America, Lincoln-Bar, George Washington Club, Nuits de Houston, Pittsburgh-Pigalle. "You mean whorehouses?" I asked Fils-Aimé.

"*Girl* whores," he said. "Very disease. Very boring."

I rubbed my eyes. Now I felt ready to sleep. That's a sign of unease and depression in me. The cackle of nightsounds was deafening as we drove to Pierre St.-Pierre's house. Fils-Aimé tended to cast long languishing glances against my undistinguished profile as we hurtled through the crowds on the road. I worried; I didn't doze. This perpetual slum, this lost people in their backwater of colonial history, worried me. I couldn't imagine the entrepreneur or slave-dealer, if that's what he should be called, living in one of these anthive shacks pitched along the ragged tidewaters. And of course he didn't.

There was a finger of peninsula and the highway turned. We drove into a little private road. Fils-Aimé climbed out to unhook a gate, but before he could do it, a sleepy youth with a rifle stood up among tropical garden rubble, pointed the weapon at him, made ready to shoot him for trying to do another man's work, recognized him, looked at me, nodded as if he recognized me, opened the gate, beckoned us through, returned to the bench where he did his serious dozing. He was dressed in rags and shreds, but he wore the metal-rimmed sunglasses of the airport Macoutes.

As we bounced across the ruts past the gate, the guardian held up an eight-by-ten glossy photograph of Sid Kasdan. It was dark. We moved too fast for me to recognize where it had been taken. The sensation was worse than seeing an old letter you have written, traveled through the mails to its destination, kept by someone you like less than you used to. Fils-Aimé winked at me. "Perhaps are surprise?" he inquired.

"Seldom," I said. God will forgive me this fib.

The dirt road turned under palms, mango trees, a dense stand of green, creaking bamboo with its sectional segments, and then suddenly became graveled. We stopped. A house of spaghetti and gingerbread leaned in the dark by the beach. Beyond, the bay of Port-au-Prince gleamed, oily layers of black mirrors, and a giant dark alligator hulk lay in it, visible in the moonlight, the Île de la Gonâve. I had done some of my geography homework on the flight here.

"Come," said Fils-Aimé.

"Evidently they expect us."

"Evidently they expect you," he said, not giggling now. The darkness failed to appeal to him, too. Why was the house dark? Candles burned; lamps flickered inside. He raised his hand to knock, but the .door was already being unlatched and resonant welcoming sounds were emitted by a fat, happy, deep-voiced woman. "Forgive us, the electricity, the entire quarter of Bizoton, la pauvre Haiti, forgive!"

The woman was not a woman. It was immense, it was dressed in peasant costume, a madras cloth around its head, with three knots standing crazily up; it was a man. "I am Madame Sara," it said.

"Pleased, I'm sure."

"On peut entrer?" Fils-Aimé asked.

"You also," said Madame Sara.

The air outside tasted of charcoal smoke and mangoes. I took one last breath of this dense warmth. I said good-bye to the real world for awhile.

I walked as if the floor might suddenly sag me into a pit. It was how I entered alleys off the rue de l'Amiral Guey-don in Saigon. Or Buckeye Avenue in Cleveland. I abandoned hope and did it anyway. I entered this house. That house. Inside, Madame Sara had created Paris 1900, New Orleans 1910; I might have the years slightly off, since there was also a large stereo rig next to the breakfront Zenith radio. A battery-operated Mexican picnic rig was emitting songs by a French chanteur de charme. The room was buffered with rugs, tapestries, paintings of stalwart youths, coffee and tea silver services, little coffee tables, bigger coffee tables, couches, pillows, chairs, and a selected few human beings. The bulbs on the frames of the paintings were out, but there had been bulbs. The teeth smiling at me belonged to several folks. They liked taking in my astonishment at this sudden heavy luxury, elegance, and taste (they thought it good taste, I'm sure). Grinning folks grinned at me. Maybe I grinned back.

"You are said to be a most outstanding personality," said Madame Sara.

"Not necessarily."

"I suppose you have chosen to be such."

"If I am, I've drifted into it."

"You imply? But never mind what you imply. The national drink of the Republic is rum-coca, rum-soda, and if you like local color, yes. Even clairin with the juice of Sha-dek. Otherwise I suggest scotch-rocks, martini-gin-ver-mouth, boo."

"Boo?"

"Marijuana, the leaf and stem of the Caribbean hemp plant. It has been so long since I speak American with a true native son as yourself. And now I introduce—"

Roger, Claude, Victor, Albert, Fortuné, Zissmanne. The room was filled with furniture and delightful folks, all men, only Madame Sara partly a woman, it seemed, if one judges by exterior robes. But maybe it was only a Haitian caftan. No, it was a dress.

"And now please to sit. There is tea for the thirst in the samovar. We of Haiti, of course, have no relations with Soviet Russia, but I, of course, with the great Soviet Union, since I travel to Paris and there join a party on tour, have relations."

"I see. The samovar is nice."

"Like Moog synthesizer, perhaps unique example in Haiti. But Moog is so difficult here with electricity situation, alas. You see."

"I see, alas. Our people in Frankfurt—" I had been instructed.

"I know where they are!" He rustled his skirt distractedly. His legs were covered with little black dots like ants heading for the nest. He needed a fresh shave. "Frankfurt, indeed! Please! But no business, surely, until we are friends, or if not friends, at least we are as one."

There would be no business for a long time if these were the conditions. I was determined not to pass my life learning to trust Madame Sara. On the battery radio, for some reason, a station was now playing dance music like the ballads I remembered from my boyhood in summer camp, the sounds from the resort across Big Wolf Lake, and these elegant black men were moving gracefully around the room together, dodging furniture, never once knocking anything over, doing the fox trot. The curtains and the gentle sea outside muffled the sounds of Port-au-Prince across the bay.

"I am not the most important person here," Madame Sara stated, "but I am perhaps the most ... my diction is clearest. So for the moment you will do our business with me."

There was a cold ire in that *will*. There were paper cutters and letter openers all over the room, displayed on hooks and in little scabbards. I wouldn't like to figure what was being hidden. I had seen furniture and paintings. I saw knives and daggers. Madame Sara's face was creased in smiles as she noticed that I was taking in the facts of my life here.

"Please sit, dear Sid, plèase sit."

I am a pilgrim. So far I was little more than a courier for the sellers of product. It was as if they wanted to make me ready for the real work. I drank what Madame Sara put in my hand, a sweet dark punch, rum and Coca-Cola, with an odd fuzzy penetrating icy taste. I was a pilgrim taking refreshment—

And I awoke with the sun streaming through the cracks in heavy green shades. There was a coffee service by my side, a mango sliced with lemon, eggs under a silver cover, a pitcher of hot milk, and the boy who served was just escaping down the hall. The party was over. The dancers had gone home. The fox trot was ended. It was morning and I was in a narrow iron bed with fluffy pillows and frilled sheets.

"I suppose you imagine you were drugged," said Madame Sara. "You were just very tired and too much rum, I suppose?"

His question meant, Do you think you were drugged?

"Weren't you wearing women's clothes last night?"

"Only on Tuesday evening. My name is Saloman, Saloman Saint-Jupe." He was wearing a white linen suit like that of Fils-Aimé, white shoes, peacefully hilarious smile. "Saint-Jupe means Sainted Skirt, which I think droll," he said. "A fate I was born to."

68

"Droll," I said, propping myself up like a patient and taking coffee.

"People think they are poisoned when it is only jet lag."

"I reserve comment."

"You would feel sick. You are not perfect, Mr. Sid, but you are well and refreshed."

"I feel fine. No headache. Hungry."

I felt slightly woozy, had a headache, and didn't really want more than black coffee. But what was done was done. Pilgrims must go through a progress and trials. My body was untampered with, no unexpected sore places. Perhaps I was just, as he said, tired after much voyaging and an afternoon in a tropical place. I'd ride with that one awhile.

"You enjoy breakfast, then you come with me."

"What happened to all the men who were here?"

"Last night? You remember? Excellent. Gone, all gone," he said, sighing over the nights of Madame Sara which had to end with my waking up on his guest bed, covered with a loose-knitted shawl.

"Okay," I said.

"Surely you would like a bath?"

"No, I'm ready."

With downcast reproachful eyes he said, "The bath is ready. I will leave you for a moment."

I climbed into a deep Japanese wooden tub. It was more like sit or kneel. A large white fluffy towel was suspended just outside the tub, waiting for me. This was no aerodynamic miracle, since it was suspended from the arms of a boy who solemnly held it there until I was ready for it, and then sought to envelop me in his ten-year-old arms. I used the towel, not the towel boy; sent him away; perhaps I was doing everything wrong. The hard life of a pilgrim includes many temptations.

Sara-Saloman waited, tapping a heavy stick. "Coco-macaque," he said, "for wild beasts, burglars, bandits, etcetera. Many of the creatures I hit with my coco-macaque are etceteras." The car was a rusty Chevie with a bumper sticker reading *Sports Club of Ft. Lauderdale*. "We call it a Bogotá," he said, "because legend tells that all old Haitian automobiles come from Colombia." This Bogotá had a chauffeur, the same ten-year-old who had sought to dry me after my bath. He sat on a pile of old almanacs and could see over the dashboard pretty well. "Fils-Aimé sick, fever," said Saloman. "Sometimes I worry."

I could hear the city, long-awakened, waking up again for me. I could hear the dogs and chickens and babies and the knocking of hammers. The honking of car horns filled my head. The heat washed in with the noise. I wondered if Fils-Aimé had passed on his fever when he kissed me (he didn't kiss me) and I felt my forehead to see if it was hot. I couldn't tell. In dust and clangor we circulated. When we stopped for donkeys in the road, peasant heads pressed to the windows of the Bogotá to see if we were anyone they knew. Saloman with our ten-year-old driver was taking me someplace.

"Actually," he said, "actually, in fact, there seem to be people who never sleep. It is as if the city does not sleep. Even during the bad times with Papa Doc and the Macoutes, there were people outdoors at night. Those, of course, whose lives do not matter to themselves or anyone else. Those who study the gods by moonlight. Those sorts, plus a few sharks and leopards."

We drove. Black goats with garbage and shit clotted in their beards, jackal-like dogs, frantic little pigs running like dogs, chickens cleaning up the booty of other creatures. In the pools and ditches by the side of the road I thought I saw toads, frogs, narrow scavenger fish, spiders who walk on water, a water jungle to rival this city swamp.

"Whoever, hearing the sounds of shooting in those days, would stay outdoors and not go back into his house? Yet

70

some did," said Saloman. "I still think about this important fact, and that is why I choose to help my young men escape this beautiful country where life is so hard, so impossible. I remember the troubles and I think: This young man, that young man, he has a chance in New York, Beverly Hills, even Chicago, where there is not so much shooting in the streets."

"Which young men? How do you make your arrangements?"

"The family, the parents, the young man himself is the ultimate authority, my friend. But life, the ardors of a difficult life, is the *ultimate* authority. And of course a moving spirit, whom you must know as I know him; a fine North American person of integrity and impeccable credentials. Which is, of course, where we go now."

Ah. Then there was a point to this voyaging. And Saloman was only an agent, perhaps the Haitian who cleared tax and export duties with the local authorities, but American know-how organized the trade. Things unfolded slowly, but they unfolded.

"This street," he said, "is named the Boulevard of the Aristocrats, boulevard des Aristocrates." It was a dusty hell slash near the Iron Market, in the portside chicken scratch and jackal destruction of the city. We could barely move. The Bogotá stopped and we pushed through the crowd. No one looked to see whose elbow or knee jammed the next person. The street was filled with flesh, sick, dying, and even well; and a noise, and a scream, and a clatter, and a shout. Animals don't live like this, nor insects; but perhaps a paramecium swarm, breeding in fetidness, invisible to the eye, might resemble under a microscope this squirming agitation. Look closer: Those are faces. Look closer: human beings. I thought I saw a blue dog with a pointy muzzle, but it was some kind of fierce pig from the Boulevard of the Aristocrats, a sinewy, muscular porker.

The stench. I have a strong stomach.

"Our Boulevard of Millionaires, some call it," Saloman remarked.

A colonial building with an immense wooden door locked with an iron crosspiece. Here the governor might enter with his carriage. A man in jeans, no shirt, guarded it. When Saloman raised his hand to knock, the man raised his fist warningly. It is my job to do the knocking, the raised arm declared.

"You know me," Saloman said in French.

"Madame Sara."

The naked black arm with the grayish, dusty fist knocked, his twin brother inside unlatched as he slid the bolt, and the door creaked open. We entered a coolness. There were long tables under snaking networks of fluorescent lights. Young men were gluing colored glass bits to colored glass bits, separated by lead—what the devil?—and then I saw the finished Tiffany lampshades piled in the corner.

"Come," said Saloman.

In another room, weavers, the clicking of looms. In another, mahogany carvers. In another, painters painting country scenes on screens. In another, a pile of fishhooks and nobody present. We walked through this series of silent rooms, young men silently working, until an office which said:

HORACE WORTHINGTON, *President.*

The guards must be triplets. A third identical brother guarded this door. Unlike the others, he wore a shirt, a starched and ironed J. Press white button-down collar shirt, over his jeans. His feet were bare and his toes stubby. He didn't have to knock; perhaps we were expected; he opened the door with a courteous bow.

I looked at my host, standing tricky-angled and smiling, and thought: I'm supposed to be a pilgrim, that's what I tell me, I'm in quest for distraction, I was very sad ... Then how do I find myself in the office of this skinny, pale, scrubbed, pink, white-suited—another white linen suit!— little entrepreneur. His first word was: "Tiffany."

"Kasdan, Sid Kasdan," I said.

He showed lovely teeth, white and even, when he laughed. He laughed easily. "No, my name isn't Tiffany. Tiffany is my main task in the shop. My name is—would you believe it?—January Worthington. Which I think ridiculous, my mother *doomed* me with that name, but I outwitted her, I call myself Jan."

"How do you do, Mr. Worthington."

"Jan."

"Okay."

"You're occasionally very polite, Mr. Kasdan."

"What are you asking of me?"

"Why are you here?"

"I ask that myself a lot. I've been asking that all over the world these days."

"Only the Western world, of course."

"You have other plans for me?"

He wore rings, but no gold chains. He was dressed like a Boston banker in Palm Beach for the winter—no, like the eccentric son of that banker. White linen suit and wide flowered tie. I imagined someone being shut up alive and bricked over. It was what happened to me when my wife left. I felt like dying; I couldn't breathe. That seems to be the way to get on in the world. Once you're dead, you can do almost anything. And that's what I was doing.

Said Jan Worthington, "You are running away, of course, but you are not a criminal. There is no record on you. Oh, a little misdemeanor felony. Almost no record.

You are almost respectable. Such is a considerable advantage from our point of view."

"So far I've not done anything very useful. Frankfurt doesn't count."

"You've been interested? Boredom and anxiety relieved by a certain variety and risk? I mean to serve men's needs, Sid."

The man made his decisions from evidence. Maybe he could even understand about the wedding band I had left in the glove compartment of the car I sold because it reminded me of her. I had forgotten about the ring. I had bought and worn it to please her. My fidelity, I had thought, might please her. I had not forgotten the ring in the glove compartment. Jan was watching me carefully. He sighed. "Poor boy," he said. "You are like me in some respects—"

"Less elegant, less slim, less rich, less sure of himself—"

"Yes. Less successful, of course. I am more effeminate. You're kind of butch. Albeit less hunky, I am more comfortable in my skin." He was totaling up some kind of character summary. "You cling to your old fantasies about women and how they make you sad, make you happy—"

"Mostly sad, I admit it."

"So you don't lie to yourself."

"I do. I mean I cling to memories."

"To fantasies. No matter. You believe she held the key to happiness. That was very, oh, very girlish of you, Sid. A number does that, my friend." He held up his pale slim paw with its exquisite cuticles and nails. "Don't argue the point with me, I'm not interested. In any case, no one wins debates. You have un côté de réaliste, also, and that makes you more useful for my purposes. It saves you. A little." He stopped. He was pleased that I saw no need to defend myself. He appreciated not being interrupted. "I was very well informed about you from the beginning, Sid. It would be foolish of me to rush in with an intuition that you are exactly perfect. You are not exactly perfect, and alas, few people are. My brother sometimes thinks he is, but he is not. My sister. It's a family trait. You were unaware we did a careful check, I suppose. We spent months. A colleague you didn't know. We spent money. His reports were tragic to read. I believe pathetic is the better word. You were so weary, my friend. Your alertness was temporarily absent—" He smiled inquisitively, as if deciding from my face whether to yawn or shrug. A little of both "—I trust only temporarily. Due to your problem, women, and about two-thirds of civilized men still suffer from the same foolishness. Only a few of us are straight with ourselves."

"I didn't expect, here, to have doctrine argued at me and what is straight."

"We're just gossiping, Sid, two gentlemen in a difficult business far from home." Coffee had appeared, little white porcelain cups, a large silver thermos with a cork top. It looked familiar. But everything was strange.

He poured and graciously handed me a cup. His eyes up close were blue and boyish, with networks of sun wrinkles surrounding them. "Who crosses me," he said cheerily, "since I'm so sure of myself—sugar? Not cream, I hope."

"No cream."

"Who crosses me I'll kill. Or perhaps, if I am too busy, my brother Horace will do it."

**13** Perhaps it was now time to consider what I was doing, where I was heading, why the end of a marriage had brought me to the Port of Princes, but I have the impression—a mark of stymied philosophy, I suppose—that my whole life has consisted of an attempt to take stock. Now, past the middle of my life, to arrange everything in order on the shelves seems an act of either excessive modesty or arrogance. I run away in order to face the facts. How could this be so? Well, my life is still not done, which is also arrogance. I think I'm a boy with a future. And nothing is worth clinging to anymore: That's no boy with a future.

Even my wife had the additional burden of being a stock-taking instrument. I was beginning to take her side against me.

So this neat, skinny, elegant American, Jan Worthington, in his linen suit and his clear nail polish, is both a dealer in fresh Tiffany glass and a murderer? Or maybe not. But if a murderer, of whom? Why? For what whim? (And if not, why that look of killing in his smile-suffused blue eyes?)

Perhaps I don't give enough importance to money. Since I had an ex-wife, I didn't need greed.

Jan Worthington and I were making a business trip to the market in Kenscoff, a village dropped from birds' wings high in the cool mountains above Port-au-Princc. I thought Fils-Aimé would come for me in his car, his own white suit. Instead, my caller was Jan Worthington himself. (Did he think me important when even I placed little value on myself?)

Fils-Aimé came, too. He trotted up the stairs of the Grand Hotel Oloffson to get me. He brought me down past the little bongo-playing band, guitar, pipes, tonsils; past Dr. Vincent, the voodoo priest and seller of primitive paintings at bargain prices; past the loitering guides and drivers and pimps and tourists out for a little daring, harmless breathing.

"Thank you," said Jan. "Now you may go."

I slipped into a black Mercedes sedan. It seemed that Fils-Aimé was staying behind at the Oloffson bar. Sometimes Jan Worthington liked to drive, and this was one of those times. Upward on twisting roads, we drove in a low gear through the cooling city toward Bourdon, Petionville, higher, and the temperature dropped steadily as the diesel motor worked. My friend hummed to himself. He looked alert, like a man who enjoyed himself and what he was doing. This should have inspired confidence in me and didn't. Because he was so interested, I pretended to be sleepy. He didn't mind. He drove. He put down the window and breathed an air of eucalyptus and flowers. Despite myself, I too enjoyed the mountain lifting us into the cooler sky like an elevator.

"Awake?" he asked.

"Yes."

"Sleepy?"

"Not very."

"Good. Then listen." He recited to me what sounded like a poem. "Grasped by the Burning Fierceness of Tropical Climate, She Plunged Into Sensualities of All Sorts."

Quite naturally I responded with: "What?"

"I like to say this plaque about Pauline Bonaparte, who lived for a time in Haiti."

"That helps."

"It's my little say-a-poem. We are all similarly grasped here, my friend."

"Is that what grasps you?"

"Not entirely. Money. Adventure. Boys. What grasps you also grasps me, Sid."

"That's not my story, as I try to keep explaining."

"Don't I listen? Perhaps not. I'd rather you lived up to my idea than be obliged to live up to yours. It's a Worthington trait you may have noticed. So I don't pay too much attention to what you say." And he gazed sidelong at me with nicely crinkling, sociable, ice-blue eyes. I remembered other things he said. Although slim and clean, he would fight nastily if it lay in his interest to do so.

In the village of Kenscoff there was a fresh smell of eucalyptus and vegetable gardens. A stream jumped from rock to rock and crossed the road under a plank bridge. The breathing was cheerful here after the dense hothouse of Port-au-Prince. Chickens and dogs printed their tattoos on the mountain air, and there was also a rhythm of drums and chanting. Imagine this travelogue plus onions. I liked being alive here with Jan Worthington. For a millisecond I thought of being here with Priscilla.

"This coumbite," Jan said, "cooperative work rite, folk ritual, they get together for a house-raising, picturesque, folkloristic, nice singing and dancing, somebody plays the pipe, another the whistle, the drums, lovely people with lovely bodies, white teeth flashing—"

"You've done this for tourists before."

"How many times. Oh, how many times, Sid. No, this time it's clearing the field, you see, over there, that hillside, of rocks. What a sweet lad that admiral is." He was looking at a boy, naked except for cut-off jeans, blowing a Marine whistle in time to the drumming. "Admiral of the coumbite," said Jan, "blows a sweet whistle. They smell like fresh onions up here. They grow them, they eat them, they smell like them. You've never buried your nose in something so good, Sid."

"May I be the judge of that?"

"Try."

"You make it sound nice, I'll say that for you."

"You want one?"

No, but I loved the chanting, and the sight of the little group working in unison like a centipede over the steep hillside, sharing the labor, assigning the tasks of making music, whistle, bamboo pipe, drum, to ease the labor into pleasure. Shiny black peasant faces. A mist from the forests of Furcy, farther up and up the mountain.

"Nice," said Jan Worthington. I was about to agree; then he said: "He's nice."

"What are you looking for?"

"I know the answer to that and so do you. The question should be: What are *you* looking for?"

I strolled down the road to the little store, a couple of boxes under a leaf roof, chewing gum and individual cigarettes for sale, hot pork wriggling in a pan over a fire in a steel box, eyes following the blanc. Jan's eyes followed him, too, and smiled. Well, I don't like not being the master of my fate. I put myself in this condition. I chose it. But choosing it doesn't make me its master.

"Come," said Jan, following me. "Let us not quarrel, my friend. I was born in Boston, where we are diplomats, and live in Haiti, where I survive most adequately in the heat by avoiding pain and strain. Truce. Truce, please, dear friend."

At the little hotel where we stopped for dinner there was a garden with dense bougainvillea, ferns, mango trees, a fig tree, little bushes which, it seemed, were coffee trees. It was a thick cool summer evening, like a night from my summers as a boy. I didn't recall this feeling of ease during the intervening years. Thank you, Jan. There were beautiful slim girls in white dresses, chattering over tall glasses, with sexy sly eyes. A radio played a merengue. The girls were black. Well, that wasn't the music of the radios of my childhood, nor were those the girls, and it didn't matter. I drank coffee, nothing more. Nearby I could hear murmurings of peasant women wading in the stream, and from its banks arose the smells of leeks, tomatoes, burning charcoal, fresh water; soft laughter all around.

I walked out behind the hotel garden. The women were frying little darting freshwater fish on rocks in open fires by the stream. They scooped the fish out and flung them like popcorn onto the rocks and picked them up with their bare fingers, all for the fun of it, I suppose.

I could be happy here.

The longer a man lives, the wider the ripples of memory which stir the waters about him. I had never been here. I was happy, and there was also the echoing silence of loneliness for where I had already been.

"Enough of that," a familiar voice said, and I turned, and Worthington was standing there with a pistol in his hand.

"What the devil's that?"

"I am now ready to ask you to do something you don't want to do."

"Oh come on, friend, come off it."

The pistol stub didn't move or waver. "I know what I'm doing."

"What makes you think that will convince me about anything?"

"I'm interested not the least in your thoughts. Your thoughts, well, it's your business. But I can convince your acts."

"I doubt it."

"I'm sure of it . . . Stop moving."

I knew he wasn't drunk. Perhaps it was coke that gave him the pink nostrils and icy clarity. I thought to grab him, hit him over the head with the butt. If it was a joke, he deserved this punch line. But I saw from how his red-rimmed eyes followed me that I would get a bullet in the face before I could touch him.

"Do you have a license for that thing?" I asked.

"I have a Haitian license. It's what applies here. Says I can only kill snakes, wild animals, burglars, etcetera. You're an etcetera."

I had heard this before from Saloman about the coco-macaque. They were escalating the weaponry around here. The sounds of the partying mountainside suddenly were different. Was this really good-bye? No, no, I wasn't ready yet. I asked, "What do you want?"

"A natural act."

"What?"

"From you, Sid. What you would call an unnatural act."

"Are you kidding?"

"Right here. Right now. In this lovely garden."

He could kill me, he would, he would do it willingly, and yet I thought it a joke. My death might be a waste, or at least an interruption, but still this moment seemed unreal and a comedy. Shouldn't there really be some lust and rage in the Boston diplomat's heart? One doesn't perform such an act out of calculation, does one? "But I hardly know you," I said.

"You'll know me better."

"And afterward you'll have to keep a gun on me till I leave the country."

"I'll take that chance."

"Are you really so much in love, my friend?"

"There are other reasons."

"Do they require this?"

He kept the gun on me. He unzipped his pants. He let

them fall. He was wearing silk panties, woman's panties, of the sort some movie actors are said to find most comfortable for a man in motion. What he revealed was limp.

I stood there in silence. He was testing, but I didn't know what he wanted to find. I wouldn't try to figure him out. Now and here, I'd only do what I wanted to do. I stared at him as unconcernedly as if I were reading the small print in someone else's newspaper.

He began to laugh, he pulled up his pants, he put the gun away, he said, "My son. Good for you. Forgive my little joke."

"You're a serious man," I said.

"I like to get involved only with people who keep their wits about them and don't perform rash stunts. You believed I was ready to kill you and you were right. I admire good judgment, my friend."

"Not funny."

"Come. I'll buy you a rum-coca."

I felt the blood rushing to my face. "Let me tell you something, mister. That's an asshole game. I don't appreciate it. I think I'll take back that you're serious. What you do is serious, but maybe you're just an ordinary slave trader—"

"Oh come along, Sid. I said I'm sorry, didn't I? I meant to."

"—or you're just playing asshole games for the fun of it."

"You're having an adrenalin reaction, Sid. I'm truly concerned. Would you like me to get on my knees to you?" And he did. A spatter of dust arose from the plank. He tumbled and folded his hands in front of my belt.

I moved off and laughed and he stood up, slapping at the smudges on his knees. "That's better. Be a good friend and colleague. I do hate a dirty linen suit, don't you? Come on, we'll have a rum-coca and then we'll get on with it." He touched my shoulder but quickly removed his hand. No offense meant. He said quickly, very businesslike, "We

82

have two sorts of farms in this country. Boys grow wild in the mountains, as here in Kenscoff. And we also cultivate them in hothouses. We can pick the wild ones in the mountains, but the cultivated ones are tamer. So tomorrow I want you to make another business trip with me, okay?"

"I'm not sure I want to."

"Are you afraid of me? Are you still having this problem with your adrenalin?"

"I'm not afraid to die. I'd rather avoid trouble about it, though."

"You're supposed, by this time, to be afraid of me. That's the normal thing."

"I'm normal, Jan."

"You're also supposed to be both alert and efficient. And calm inside."

"I said I'm normal. You ought to know what you're buying. Couldn't I just walk off?"

He grinned and blew a kiss through the cool air, his lips puckered, his eyes alert slits of amusement. "Normal," he said. "Well, you can't help yourself. No, you couldn't just walk off. I wouldn't let you. You *couldn't*, Sid. I would stop you with apologies you can't believe. I would speak of adrenalin reaction. I'd give you pituitary if it got serious. I would actually fall to my knees, Sid, and kiss you all over. I would, oh, I don't know, I'd find so many ways to apologize and make you smile and purr and just, oh, intrigue a man like you who has gone through such a hard time lately with his life and all. Sid. Poor Sid. This *is* dangerous. I know it is. That's why we want you and that's why you want it, too. So why don't you just relax and enjoy the fun?"

He examined me carefully, a specimen he wanted thoroughly to understand.

"I'm so glad we've had this little talk, a chance to get to know each other. I hope you'll forgive that we will have some passengers on the trip back to town, Sid."

**14** When we drove back down the winding mountain road toward Petionville, the hillside suburb of Port-au-Prince, the back seat held three lads—Jan's word for them—giggling and sucking sugar cane with loud popping noises between their lips, until Jan suddenly said, "Here! Civilize yourselves!" and reached into the glove compartment and pulled out a box of New Orleans Sugar Pops, lollypops on plastic stems, sold to dentists, pediatricians, and health-care professionals who deal with children, according to the instructions on the box.

Jan stopped the Mercedes at a gully where goatskins were stretched out on a line, half-cured, waiting to be sold to tourists. He waved away the Madame Sara who ambled up, smoking her clay pipe. "Now throw that filth out the window." He meant the stringy stalks of sugar cane. They did. "That's better. Now try some American sugar." The automobile slid back onto the road. "We start with basics. We start to educate them very gently. Most of these lads never got to taste refined sweets before, much less saccharin. Lick gently, lads!" he called back cheerily in English. They didn't understand the language, but they got the idea. Not a one of them crunched up his sugar pop. They licked like champions.

Behind the square of Petionville—church, the Choucoune nightclub, gingerbread houses, a few stores selling colored sweet drinks and American canned peas and corn flakes and fresh vegetables carried down from Kenscoff in baskets on the heads of market women—the road ceased to be paved as if by a sudden will to go native. It was a tropical path. Well, the town wasn't so urban, either. Ruts, lurches, flying insects, and the sun of jungle mingled with the sun of town, reflected through palm leaves and off zinc roofs. I saw a broad nose the size of a donkey being pushed by a man in cut-off jeans and running with sweat. It was a papier-mâché nose, a carnival mask on a sled outfitted with wheels. He was turning the crank on some sort of pump as he pushed it, and this made the nose ooze oil, and the man wore a very serious expression of concern on his face as he practiced his nose for the carnival months ahead.

"They think life isn't serious, though they might be starving. They die of syphilis or tuberculosis or carelessness. They're right," Jan said. "Now where the hell's that path?"

One of the lads in the car looked nearly white, not the freckled pink look of the unsturdy albino, but really like a Spaniard or Brazilian. Olive. Green eyes. For Jan, a valuable product. He revolved his hand as if he were turning a pump when we passed the carnival nose. Jan stopped the car a moment at a stone wall covered with bougainvillea. We went into first gear and bumped into a driveway leading to a tall skinny spaghetti-house, carved wood and windows with shutters open and french doors. He stopped. A sign said:

The nearly white lad had curly reddish hair growing on the side of his head, not quite sideburns, and it made him look older.

Mission des Pères de Saint-Brice
*École Privée*

The boy had touched his hair back with his fingers and that was why I noticed.

Mission des Pères de Saint-Brice
*École Privée*
*Défense d'Entrée*

At the third signal we were there. A man in a red robe with a red fez came to the door, but I was looking at Jan. They were the same man. "My twin sibling," Jan murmured, smiling. "We used to change clothes to confuse the folks."

"There's another like you?"

"Not anymore. He's the bishop. I'm not a bishop."

"This is our friend," Jan said, introducing me. "Sid Kasdan. His Holy Excellency Bishop Francis Worthington. When he's in business, he's Horace."

"Very pleased," said the bishop, making a small curtsy in his red robes. I've heard robes keep you cool in a hot climate and never really believed it. But the bishop was a cool customer. He put on his glasses to look at the little huddle of boys, two black ones and one unusually light mulatto one.

"Your new students," said Jan. "Just don't let them get fat, the way you did the last crop. I brought them in slim and firm, and by the time you finished with them—"

"They could read, write, and keep themselves clean."

"Fine virtues, I'm sure, quite Christian, but they were also fat."

"The problem is what they want to eat, don't you find, sir?" he asked me. "And can you drag boys to play volleyball in this awful heat if they are not motivated to stay slim? I find not."

"Find yes, Frankie," Jan said.

The bishop and I watched Jan lead the boys into the back hallways of the great house. They followed like docile creatures. They were docile creatures. They looked a little like recruits being directed to quartermaster. They would never see the clothes they were wearing again. They were beginning their basic training. It made me think of Viet Nam, boys marching off for peculiar reasons. These boys had said yes to the reasons someone gave them.

"People mostly do what they want anyway," I said.

He sucked in his cheeks with disappointment. He did look like a prelate. "I thought you were smarter than that, sir. You are American. What they *need* to do."

I felt my face turning purple. "What they have to do. Then sometimes they tell themselves they want to—"

"And sometimes not," he sighed. "For example, I never tell myself I like what I'm doing, I *don't* like it. I just do it. And Jan, my dearest brother, he tells himself he loves it and I'm not so sure."

"Does he?"

"Since I ask the question, sir—but some cassava juice, yes?" He clapped his hands and the words rolled out in Creole. A young man in black pants, white shirt, not too clean, shambled off. "He could have gone to Palm Beach, that one, with a lovely retired soft-drink heir, but I failed with him. He didn't train. Nevertheless, I have kept him on as servant, first hoping the examples all around him would prove instructive, and finally because I became quite attached to him, poor thing."

"His failure was not complete," I said.

The bishop's glance at me was cold. He preferred to let it pass. I was hired for willingness, not tact. "Carry your refreshing glass," he said, "and I'll show you how we invest in our lads." We walked through the house. The cots on which the acolytes slept were simple, but the bowls, creams, soaps, and mirrors were luxurious. "Cleanliness is next to godliness—"

"But only next," I said.

"Nevertheless, it is the stage at which many, I should say most, of our clients in the U.S., Canada, and France demand absolute, I should say religious, rigor. In our sun of Haiti, which cleanses water and spirit and keeps the air pure, soap has not been of prime interest. It is expensive. The peasants wash frequently, scrub in the streams—for coolness, for freshness—and the sweat which rolls off their bodies carries much that is impure with it. But in industrial nations, soap is required. We teach. We also teach shaving, when necessary. Brushing the teeth." He pointed to a UNESCO poster advising, *Brossez dents*. "More delicate matters, in which we urge the use of paper rather than leaves. Would you like to see a lesson? It's rather amusing."

"No thanks."

"You are hasty and ready for judgments, I notice. But would you rather we exported the product without teaching it to wipe its behind?"

"I believe you."

The bishop shook his head. I was not so curious, perhaps not so intelligent, as he hoped. I would serve merely as transport, not as a participant in developing the business, unless I developed some better smarts. My ears were developed already. I heard a shrieking commotion in a room · down the hall. Unhurried, the bishop led me toward it. He shook the locked door. Inside, there were sounds of scuffling and yelling. He paused a moment, put his cassocked shoulder to the door, and shattered the catch. The door itself was barely splintered as it fell open. Two naked young men were fighting. They had flung soap, towels, and water all over the room. The bishop barely paused. He didn't ask what was the subject of the quarrel. He seized each young man in a hammerlock under his arm, and winking at me, smashed their heads together. It made me wince. They fell stunned to the floor.

"Mustn't dirty, mustn't splash," said the bishop. "Now clean up, please. God bless."

They were lying there, rolling and groaning. The odd thing was how they didn't resist the hammerlock, and let their heads thud together as if their reflexes were dead.

"Get mops," said the bishop. "Clean, please. Dry."

He led me away. "No use in asking what the quarrel is about," he said. "There is no justice here. We just don't want fighting and quarrels, I don't care about justice. If they steal, they should tell me. I'm the hand of god around here." And he put the tips of his fingers together and smiled with holy unction.

Jan had strolled back at the sound of the door breaking. "Ah, my dear brother," he said. "You are teaching the lads to obey in English."

"English and French are the working languages," the bishop said. "Obedience is the basic tongue."

I cleared my throat. "Is it necessary to . . . ?"

He took my arm. "Come. Let us walk. If you have read about Africa," said the bishop, "you may have heard of Albert Schweitzer."

"I have."

"And a little-known fact: that when patients got in his way in the hospital at Lambarene, lying about the paths where he strolled, doing good and relaxing, getting ideas about Bach or medicine or holiness, he would crack them on the head with his cane. He said it didn't hurt them as much as it would hurt a white man."

"I didn't know that."

"In my opinion, it hurts them just as much. But take those lads back there. They don't know how to react to the hurt. They can't hurt me. If they howl, I might beat them worse, or god bless, have someone else do it, or even expel them from the school. They wouldn't want that, now would they?"

"I suppose not."

"Since they have their hearts set on a life in Paris or New York or Las Vegas or Palm Beach or even, capital of their dreams, Hollywood." He pronounced it Hol-ly-wood, with a long drawling amusement. "If we just stroll back there now—"

We did. The two young men were cleaning up the bathroom. They didn't speak to each other. But everything was becoming neat, and they had put on clean white shirts and shorts.

"You see," said the bishop.

Other seminarians were reading in the kitchen, cleaning, shaving, idly turning the pages of picture books (were they in Idle Turning of Pages class?), lolling on the grass outside (Lolling 101?), practicing making themselves attractive in various ways for those who would find them attractive. They wore the school uniform of white shorts and white long-sleeved shirts with the sleeves rolled up. It made black and glistening skin more black and glistening. They smiled reverently as we strolled past. Surely they knew by this time about the head-knocking. They smiled. They didn't push their smiles ahead of them like carnival noses. They smiled with genuine affection for us, who hardly merited it.

"We, my brother and our colleagues and I, are taking them away from their sad lives in poor, forgotten Haiti,"

90

said the bishop. "Here there is only disease, poverty, desolation—you have seen the Boulevard of Millionaires, for example. Some of them will return from, say, Palm Beach with money to marry their sweethearts, buy a house, raise their children, even send them to school."

"And they will speak English by that time."

"Of course. They will remember with fondness the men who educated them. First me, and then him. We will lose a few to vice, to crime, to the immigration authorities. Some die or disappear, which is the same as dying. God bless." He sighed. "If this were not so interesting, it would not be so interesting."

I heard another duck squabble of quarrel in the kitchen where we had left some boys cooking, doing dishes, and one reading at the table. The bishop stopped. He tilted his head to listen with his good, hairy ear. Off the wall he plucked a large leather whip with insectival waving thongs. Brisk in his cassock, skirts hissing, he headed for the kitchen. I followed, though I was sure he needed no protection from my sort. That was not my job here. Perhaps he knew that I was both more curious and more intelligent than I seemed.

Okay, he knew me pretty well. I would go along on their ride to someplace strange. But even if I was a trader myself, I kept a secret from these businessmen in cassocks. The one who refused their discipline would not be forced by me.

"Excuse me if I hurry," said the bishop, "but come along quickly. This may be interesting." He smiled winsomely, wetting a thong with his tongue. "And isn't interesting what you like and need, my dear colleague Sid?"

**15** In the silence of a Petionville garden we were packed to leave. I had charge of a squad of four lads with neat straw suitcases and no trail of extra belongings. They carried uniform black vinyl folders containing passports, visas, shaving equipment, a snapshot of their home villages, and whatever toys or trinkets they could cram in them—perhaps combs and ballpoint pens to trade with the savage natives of Manhattan or Las Vegas. I kept their airline tickets in my briefcase. I had my instructions.

They were going to the U.S. to work in Mr. Jan Worthington's Tiffany glass and weaving enterprises. They were trainees. They qualified for student visas.

I would not beat them, but I could threaten them.

In their confusion, they would be docile. Precedent shows this. They understood. Their minds were adequate. They were skilled in grace, smiles, agreeable bending to the will of another, and retained the flashpoints of lust or anger which could light up all this amiability, as it does in what used to be considered the best of women. I remembered a girl in Paris, Hamburg, New York, and I remembered my wife, and remembered them only dimly. I was turning into a mule.

That may not have been correct. It was what, at that moment, I needed. Not needed to do. Needed to be.

I imagined being met at Kennedy Airport by a group of careful shoppers, saying, I'll take this one . . . all right, this one . . . and a week of this one.

It would not necessarily be correct. It would be what they needed to do and to be.

"Bon voyage! God bless."

We said good-bye to Jan and Francis, in his brilliant red robes, at the school in Petionville. M. Fils-Aimé, smiling in a white suit like Jan's, would drive us to the airport in the air-conditioned Mercedes belonging to Jan, and he waited, so glad to see us all, so happy, so lounging, while I shook the hands of the twin entrepreneurs. Jan was the one in white linen, straw hat, white shoes, white socks, very much in white.

I slid into the front seat with Fils-Aimé. The palest of the four lads, Lucien his name was, hesitated a moment, but managed to notice (tact lessons) that I didn't want him in beside me. He crowded in, using the jump seat, with the other three. Then he forgave me with a long slow look full of thought as I settled beside Fils-Aimé, who discoursed on Haitian history—brave poor lost people, so proud, so proud—and the difficulties of earning a decent American living in this crumpled swatch of island.

I was doing the job, and the job was doing to me what I needed done: to forget her. I wondered if those accumulating early strands of gray in her hair had taken away her pale reddish-blond fireplace glow. I wondered if she had learned to make love without making jokes afterward. I wondered if she ever thought of me.

But the most important thing about what I was doing was that I was not wondering if the telephone might ring and her voice say: It was all a mistake, I still want you, I really always did, I want you again . . .

And so I went along for this ride. Lucien was watching

me curiously. My lips must have been moving. I talked to her in my head until I could stop. His glance stopped me. Safe again.

"Ah, Meester Sid," Fils-Aimé was saying to me. "Our life is to go up and down the mountain, is it not? Is it not odd of Haiti, the fate of a Haitian person, that I so much prefer to go up the mountain than down? Do you not think this?"

"I'm sure you're right," I said.

"Ah, I am sure you are not listening to me. But for you this is a new beginning and you are thinking to your life ahead, please. So you are correct not to listen to merely Fils-Aimé, Meester Sid. Most absolutely correct ... On your right, you see Ravine of the Intoxicated."

The road took a sharp turn, the guard rail was a white strip painted along the edge, the hill fell off into a trickling streambed. I imagined the mountain people coming here for salvage every morning.

The smells of things growing alongside the mountain streams gave way to dust and charcoal smells, and then dust, tobacco, sweat, at His Excellency Dr. François Duvalier International Airport, where the noise and confusion made me long for the conveyor tubes and space capsules of Seattle. The lad Lucien hid himself behind his olive mask. He was watchful and fearful. He was saying nothing. I could see him as a pretty hood on Polk Street in San Francisco, or on the meatrack in Washington Square, or as a scared young man anyplace. He might bite, but he hid his teeth.

Amid the dense radiation of tropical bodies and a mob clamoring for attention from bureaucrats slowly, stolidly, wielding their rubber stamps, a broken loudspeaker crackled with the opposite of public address: private chaos. An eighteen-year-old cop, covered with humid dew, a rich crop of wet on the flanges of his nose, aimed his stamp and fired. A robust taxman put the airport exit tax in a box destined to good works by Mme. Duvalier Mère, "La Veuve Sainte."

Fils-Aimé sped us through the customs inspection. He took all our papers and disappeared. I stood with the four lads. Then he returned and we were ushered through a room freshly labeled VIP Courtoisie S. E. J.-C. Duvalier, which gave onto the chickenwire fence near the plane. A sign in English stated, *Haiti Welcome the Business Revolution.*—S. E. JEAN-CLAUDE DUVALIER, PRESIDENT-FOR-LIFE. We boarded. Heat, heat along the chickenwire pen, and then a blast of friendly American air conditioning from Boeing equipment. It smelled like indoors during a hot spell in New York: hometown dehydration. Abruptly my sinus was disconnected. I looked out the window and Fils-Aimé was smiling and waving. Next to him stood a Haitian Air Force captain in silken gabardine, not smiling and waving. This team watches over each other.

The engines started, I felt a moment of nostalgia for Haiti and conversation with Fils-Aimé (there was life behind his giggles and Macoute shades), and suddenly someone's hand was gripping my hand. I had company by my side. It was Lucien, who murmured in French, "Airplanes frighten me."

"Have you ever been in one before?"

"No."

"Then how do you know?"

"I have dreamed of them so often."

"Why not try another dream?" But my hand was clutched by this fear I didn't believe in. He wanted something, he dreaded something, even if it wasn't airplanes at the center of his desire. He did not want to give up his past for his future. I pulled my hand away.

"I have a question to ask." He was smiling. His teeth were large, squarish, even. He was still gripping my arm.

Maybe he wasn't frightened of the jet flight, but someone who sought the comfort of an elbow. "Tell me, sir. How would you briefly describe a slave?"

It occurred to me that Lucien might pass for white—Greek, Arab, Italian, Portuguese—in New York. This thought was not required in Haiti, but it came to mind here as we took altitude above that place. "I assume you have chosen this adventure for yourself," I said.

He listened carefully. He waited to be sure I had finished. "Do I know what will happen when I arrive someplace I have never been? I am weak, I am tempted, sir. I was captured, perhaps, by promises. How do you define slavery, if you refuse to define a slave?"

"You've been to school. Captured by promises?"

"I learned to read and write. I read a great deal—you have seen the boys under the streetlamps? That was me. And I have an excellent memory for what I read and hear. For example, I hear very distinctly that you will not tell me what is a slave."

"That's not my job."

He grinned and put his face near mine. It was smooth and clear, with only the beginnings of beard. His lips pursed up. "Then let us kiss and hug, sir. Is that your job?"

With a jerk I got my elbow out of his hand. I leaned the other way in my seat. He shrugged. He picked up the *In Flight Magazine* and began to read an advertisement for duty-free perfume and brandy in the Curaçao duty-free shopping center. Suddenly he looked up again. The advertisement did not hold his interest. He stared across the seat at me and, grinning, asked, "Hey, meestair, meestair! Ees evair-body tween? You tween M. Fils-Aimé, meestair?"

I read my magazine and believed firmly that I was coming to the end of this road. The Worthingtons didn't know it, all my new friends and dear colleagues in Europe and America thought I was only at the beginning, even I hadn't known it. I had thought I was passing the time in an agreeable way. I had thought I might have some unpredictable accident and die and that too might be agreeable. But I had not put to myself the simple question which this pretty Haitian young man had asked me: Do I know what slavery is and am I a trader in slaves?

No sweat. Not a surprise. Nevertheless it gave me the idea that I should go into retirement again. I would bring them to Kennedy Airport in New York, deliver them to those who would be there to meet us, and collect what was due me or at least what I could collect. But no, Lucien, I was not the twin of Fils-Aimé. Again I was drifting into easy decisions.

Then I had a vision of being alone for a few days in, say, Las Vegas; alone, and then with a carhop or a rich and not too old woman I would meet at the Sands or the Sahara; and I would not be twisting my soul like a tapeworm out of my body, as I was doing now, alone in a seat near Lucien, where I could feel the heat of his body, despite the steady pump of air conditioning and my will not to feel it.

I could not make the decision not to know that this young man was terrified. Lucien was about to be stuffed like an insect by a collector in Palm Springs. The other boys would be used by other collectors.

Through the thrumming of the jet engines, metal strings shivered. "Hey, guitar," I said to the stewardess.

I looked back. It was a North American kid in a dirty blue-jean suit.

The stewardess wrinkled her little nose at me. "He paid for an extra seat to keep his guitar with him like that."

"This is America, isn't it?" I asked, but wondered if the kid would be arrested at customs. Instead of me. Because the guitar might be stuffed with dope and Lucien wasn't yet stuffed.

"You staying in New York?" the stewardess asked. "I

just lay over there and I don't have much to do in that town. Nothing much happening in New York, you know?"

"Not like Memphis," I said.

"Howja know? You been to Old Town? Ain't it a pisser? You dig Dixieland?"

She had frosted hair, blond streaks painted on it, small eyes with beaver darkening around them, and a white-lipped mouth to match the frosting. Her hair was shortened regularly and professionally and clipped close as a poodle and patted in tight beside her skull. I didn't like her looks. Also I wanted a piece of her and she wanted a piece of me. But they were different pieces.

"I bet you know some good places in New York," she said.

"I bet we both do," I said.

When I feel like this, the world is not very nice. Neither am I.

**16** "Vacarme," said a dignified Haitian gentleman, proudly hoisting his belly before him, medical magazines in Spanish and German under his arm. The word this portly trilingual doctor pronounced is a French word that means hullabaloo and hurly-burly. It comes to mind at airports. The noise of customs in New York was a tropical one with the dust and humidity precipitated out by air conditioning. We were shoved and pushed into different lines. I had my instructions about the four young men, but I was still worried. One kept touching his gray thumb to his mouth as if he wanted to suck it. A superior smile was pasted on Lucien's olive-pale face; here was a young man accustomed to international travel and to the elegant manners born. The smile did not engage his eyes. The bluish color beneath the skin was fatigue. The person within was watching from far below. He was silent about his confusion.

The straw bags of tourists and Haitian visitors were opened and poked through by Irish and Italian customs inspectors who wished they were doing something else, maybe glamorous crop-dusting.

The boy with the ticket-bearing guitar was met by an

English valet, who said, "Welcome home, sir," taking the very thought from my mouth. I too was met. Three men in IBM black suits, white shirts, narrow ties, with little briefcases. "Pierre is mine." "This one is GiGi? Come with me." "Hi, I'm for that one. He looks a little tired, doesn't he? Is that one Fortuny?"

They were delivery men. I was the international courier, but they made the local deliveries, except for Lucien. I had a letter which told me to deliver Lucien to an individual—that's what it said, "an individual"—who would reach me at the Ingleside Inn in Palm Springs, California. I wasn't taking silly orders all the time. Not me. I wouldn't just get on a plane now and fly to California. No. I would spend the night in the Hilton here at the airport and then fly to California.

The very clean IBM who had come for Pierre had a shaved neck, five o'clock shadow of sandy sideburns, and very bad breath. Everything was scrubbed but his teeth, mouth, throat, and tonsils. I believed he was not the delivery man after all; he was the buyer. He was only dressed up like a delivery man. He was starting his thrills early.

I handed him a sheet of paper, and he looked surprised. "Sign," I said.

"What's that for?"

"Receipt."

"That's not part of the whole deal," he said, dog's stench blowing.

I grinned at him. "Then sign a false name." He didn't like this joke. "If you don't like it, write back to the factory in Port-au-Prince," I said. "You're John Doe, aren't you?"

"Come on, Pierre," he said.

"You want out of here," I said.

He looked at me as if he sure did. An invisible poison cloud filled the air between us. Unlucky Pierre. Pierre did not look at me at all. Well, I hadn't paid him much attention, either.

"Plans for the evening. We go."

It seemed we were all a part of the Worthington army, and we were training for the future, and now we each had a tiny job to do. But this was not the army and I had my own job to do. Forget, forget.

I'd eat an American Credit Card Club Sandwich and drink a drink of martini, help me know I'm back, and sleep in a nonmoving place with no mosquitoes and read the *New York Times*. Home at last. That's my cover story. I'm a white businessman, just doing my white job. I'm glad to be home. I would kiss the earth of the Airport Hilton except there is no such and my baggage, Lucien here, might sneeze at my behind and embarrass me.

What's this? Stuck in my raincoat pocket was an envelope addressed to a woman in Port-au-Prince. It was a letter from Pierre. Now why didn't he just ask if I'd mail his letter for him? Didn't he take a chance that I wouldn't? I would. It could be a very young wife or a mother or a beloved sister. I had none of the above. So in some ways Pierre had the jump on me.

Pierre was gone and very likely I'd never see him again, that traveling companion who helped me earn my keep. I wondered how much they had deposited in my Swiss bank. I didn't check, since I believed they were putting a correct amount in and I thought it better not to fake greed if I felt none. The Worthingtons, if they were the bankers, struck me as correct about money. If I asked them how much is two and two, they would giggle first, look nervously at each other, giggle again, look firmly at me, and ask: Was I buying or selling?

I asked for adjacent rooms in the busy airport hotel, filled with international business travelers, Germans, Japanese, and Arabs, diluted for charm with American computer salesman, and the clerk asked me pointedly, as if he couldn't believe my words: "You want *two* rooms for you and the gentleman?"

"Yes, two."

"We could give you a nice double." His eyes were going all google at the beauty of Lucien.

"Two singles will do."

"*Two? Singles?*" He was paralyzed by love.

I reached for a card, two cards, and handed one to Lucien. I started to show him where and how to sign, but he would know. He would even know enough not to fill in the place that said, *Automobile License Number* and *Business Affiliation.* He wrote, *Tourist,* in the latter line.

A Puerto Rican porter, overweight and overage, wheeled our bags upstairs, first to Lucien's room. I informed Lucien he was tired and could order a snack from room service and plan to get a good night's sleep. "Of course, of course, we both need some tranquillity from each other," he said.

"Never mind."

"Although certainly I have not wearied of you and of your kindness."

"Thank you very much. I'll tell you when you can go out."

And then I threw my bags on the bed, dismissed the bellboy before he could run through his speech about the air conditioning, the lights, the shower, the tip—gave him some folding money—and rinsed my hands, didn't use soap, dry after all that flying, that air of airplanes; left an ugly black smudge on a Hilton's towel, but they have strong detergents down in the bowels of Queens where the laundry is brought in on three-wheeled vehicles; and what I wanted was simply to get out of my skin.

This whole job had been about that.

Yet I wanted to escape the job, too.

So I went down to the lounge like a good multinational salesman to think about jet lag and drink myself into soft focus again.

"Ah knew. Ah jes' *knew*," she said, cute rump on a stool.

"Ah *knew* we would have to meet up again, you're such an interestin' person, so mysterious and all—"

"What's mysterious?"

She smiled, her beaver-fur eyes crinkling, the sunlines forming helter-skelter, the lashes pushed together and entangled. "Not an obvious fruit," she said.

Those were real lashes although they looked so false. It was the darkening on them. They had extender, like soy hamburger, but they were real.

"Wanna sit down?"

"Let's take a table," said the not obvious fruit, Sid Kasdan.

The waiter followed us as she carried her own coffee, tea, or harder stuff and waited for me to pay my rent on the darkest corner I could find. I asked for Rémy Martin and she made a little pout. "Sophisticate, aren't you?"

"Did you know I'd be in this hotel?"

"I reasoned it out."

"You all's accent seems to have dropped away."

"The customers like it. The airline people like it."

"You a hooker?"

"Shit no. I have this legit job. If I fuck at all, it's for fun and practice."

"Practice?"

"Practice in asking for little presents: jewelry, clothes, rent money."

We both laughed. I patted her hand. "I've got a flight out early this morning," I said.

"Then let's go upstairs," she said. "There's an elevator leaving very soon."

She stood up. I left some more money on the table. This side of America is tips.

The elevator was slow—others checking in, I guess—so I had a chance to ask her one more question. "You know the Worthington brothers?"

103

"They're not even bi," she said.

"But they asked you to keep an eye on me? Even the bodyguards have bodyguards around here?"—

She patted my hand. "Not that anyone thinks you're a kidnapper or a person who wants to go into business for himself. But who knows what you might could think of during the lonely night, Sid?"

There were sun freckles on her hand. It was a warm and moist hand. I had drunk too much coffee on the plane; the airport made me need a long hot soak; I would now get it. My friend, this nice young lady, would smile and wait. She was patient and kind. Like me, she was doing her job. She would work a few hours tonight.

She opened her purse in the elevator to look for something. She rummaged. She didn't find it. She was showing me she had no weapon there. That was her first gesture which failed to amuse me. The nonthreat amounted to a threat. It was to say she had something better which I didn't know about. She had the Worthingtons behind her.

But what she did later, after my long hot soak, finally managed to distract me. Lucky Lucien, next door, got a good night's sleep.

**17** There was a soft knocking at my door. I opened my eyes and reached across the bed. My fishing fingers found nothing. She was gone. I sat up. The bathroom door was open. She was absolutely gone.

The soft scraping and pushing, like the muzzle of an animal at my door.

She had departed without proper good-byes, like every woman I had met since I took this job, with little trace other than a towel on the floor. I should write down their names so I can remember them. I could still remember the one name I wanted to forget. I picked up the towel. Barely damp.

The persistent poking at my door would not let up until I answered it. There was a note on my pillow on Hilton stationery: *Now tend to business, please. (over)* I turned the paper over. *But that was nice.*

How the hell did she get out without waking me? Normally I'm a light sleeper. She had tuckered me out.

"Okay, okay, wait a second," I called to the nervous door.

And how the hell did I wake up both scared by this knock and by the absence of someone who was supposed to be there? It's easy. I wanted to put my arms around someone I trusted. Man's arterial system is not supposed to endure desire and fright at the same time. Man is supposed to choose ways that ease him.

Knock, knock, soft soft soft scraping knock.

What had I been dreaming of? A picture. A photograph of a woman, graceful, leaning forward away from the light, her head hidden, a glimpse of reddish-blond hair, her face hidden, shadows across her downcast face. She was nude. She was doing nothing. Was I a painter in my dream? I wanted her. I wanted just to look at this woman and admire her. Three women I had been with I had merely squeezed and penetrated and maybe gossiped with (maybe not) and I had forgotten their names. But I was making progress. The woman in my dream was not my former wife. I said that to please myself. I couldn't see who it was.

I slid out of bed, stiff in the crotch, dried stickiness, put a towel around myself, and went to answer the soft, persistent, patient scraping at my door. In my dream, I recalled, my own face and body had gone soft and I was wearing one of those tired oxidized wigs that float reddishly, rust-colored, on the shiny scalp, and now I was running my hand through my hair to make sure I was okay, I had my own hair, as I opened the door. If it was the police or something ugly, I wouldn't defend myself this time. Too tired from not being the master of my dreams or my fate. In trouble.

I opened the door and didn't care.

"What the devil are you doing?" I asked.

"I was raised in the country," he said, "but I learned to knock like a woman. I do not like to disturb unasked."

"Come in, Lucien. I ask." I grinned at him. "You don't know yet what disturbs and what doesn't disturb."

"I am innocent?"

"Hardly."

"Foolish or stupide?"

"You're just thinking too much about the part you're playing. You're a totally calculated person. There used to be women like that, there still are." I shut the door behind him. "What do you want?"

"I slept enough. I'm lonely."

He looked at my fingers hooked around the towel. My hairy legs. My toes.

"No, Lucien," I said. "I thought you were intelligent."

"I am."

"No, Lucien. So far you're clever. Clever only thinks of himself. Intelligence is capable of imagining the other person, and maybe someday you'll be there. You have a way to go. Lord, come on, sit down, I'll get dressed—sit down, sit down—I'll order some coffee and toast."

"I like muffins," he said.

We had a proper breakfast together, and then we refused the airport bus and took a cab, and then we boarded the flight heading west. We chatted now like old friends. I heard how he had learned English. He heard how I had learned French. We did not speak of my wife. He asked few questions. We did not speak of his job in Palm Springs. I was careful about the questions I asked.

We had stopped chatting like old friends because we were thinking about the questions we didn't ask. But I was easier with him by now. I was thinking less about myself. It was good of the Worthingtons to give me a job which was not too difficult for my distracted routines to manage. I might try to understand how someone as secret and as private as Lucien could sell something as personal as his body. Poverty? But he was not the only poor and pretty young man. Curiosity? A kind of lust? Was he simply victimized? I was far from knowing. I said I might try. I wondered if he cared about why I was in the business of selling him. He did not look like a man who asked many questions about

107

others. Himself, that secret self, was enough to think about.

Neither one of us touched our Port-A-Pack trays of airline lunch.

Lucien's smile, the smile of Lucien riding easy to California, vexed me. It was as if he had another eye, and it was studying his own entrails, and he was pleased by what he observed of his inner workings, even if it was only peristalsis. He had no right to be so self-possessed when he was about to be possessed by a veterinarian in Palm Springs. They said he would have dog-walking duties. The dry hot climate would not remind him of Port-au-Prince; too hot, too clean, absent of fallen fruit and humid decay. Why was this young man so tranquil? He had been olive-gray with fatigue only yesterday. Why was he so easy and pleased toward the end of his voyage?

Why did I have no such inward smiles for my own being?

It would be awkward, I thought, going through these confusions, wandering like a child in a wood while pretending to be a grownup conniver, to discover I didn't love that wife who did not love me. There was a deadness in my heart. I didn't know if it was still the old regret and sorrow or if it was simple deadness.

Along about Nebraska Lucien finally turned toward me, having tried silence over half a continent and found it excellent. He would now sample something less excellent. "Yes?" he said.

"Yes what?"

"You have been wishing to talk."

"Not particularly," I said, and that lasted us another state or two, but finally I said, "Why you? Why this? You're not normal, Lucien."

"You ask that question because you have not lived in Haiti."

"Not every Haitian boy—" he smiled and shook his head

and I decided it was a cheap shot "—not every Haitian man does what you're doing."

"No. True. But not every one has the opportunity. And you ask this question, also, because you do not live in my skin, sir."

Palm Springs dog-surgeon and cat-pediatrician was about to take lodging in parts of his skin. Lucien was smiling as if he read my thought. He seemed to have taken up American smiling as we crossed this continent.

"You mean I haven't been poor?" I asked him. He shrugged. "I am, even if not poor like you, and also I have troubles." He smiled into my eyes as if ignorance of his needs were a form of tactlessness at which he chose not to take offense. The smile was a joyous vacant beaming. "Everyone's troubles are private," I said grudgingly.

"Unless one chooses to share them."

Now it was my turn to indicate trivial response with a shrug and grin.

"Love is a choice if not a sharing," he said, "a choice to share what cannot be shared, loneliness, longing, want, even hunger and thirst and the color of skin, which probably has never been a trouble for you."

"You're very light—"

"Clear, we call it in Haiti. Clair." It sounded like a woman's name.

"You could pass, I suppose."

"Yes. Which means I have trouble because I look as if I might like to pass and trouble because I cannot."

"You're very pretty."

"More trouble."

"Intelligent, it seems."

"Has it helped you, Meester Sid, to be clever?"

"It entertains me sometimes."

"Well, me, too. But in the meantime I can get cold, hungry, tired, and killed. I know very little I can do except

109

what I am going to do. I have to forget I am I, I am Lucien, and become a pale brown thing who does what the bishop taught me to do. I am a thing. I am funny to watch. I am sexy to play with. Thank you very much, sir."

And he turned away to watch Phoenix or Tucson below. I waited. He had finished with our conversation. I didn't pick up my magazine. I didn't ask for a cup of coffee or a drink. I didn't go to the bathroom. He didn't speak to me again, he kept his face at the window, this must have strained his back and neck, until we were coming in for our landing, when he buckled his seatbelt and said: "Le pays est trop grand. La conversation est trop longue. Merci, quand même."

"I wish there were something else I could do for you."

He picked up my hand as if he were an Italian count and I a woman. He kissed the air near my hand. "Haiti is Haiti and America is America and you are you and I am I."

"Okay."

"But in our case, dear keeper, black is white and white is black."

The village of Palm Springs, home of Dwight David Eisenhower, Frank Sinatra, Gerald Ford, and Spiro T. Agnew at times, home of movie stars on weekends and the allergists from Denver who own condominiums, realtors from Chicago who buy and sell the condos, lies at the end of a long flight from New York's Kennedy Airport. I was sitting beside Lucien, wondering what else he made of America. If I asked him, he might say, with that blank intelligent grin, Opportunity. America had been created by men like him, although their tasks and services were different ones.

At the end of the flight, at the village jet airport, a dog trainer named Dr. Gilbert Bonni would be meeting us. I imagined a heavy Dodge station wagon with wire mesh to keep the dogs from jumping on the front seat. We landed.

It wasn't a station wagon which seemed to have permission to slide near the runway along with the county police. *No Parking. Towaway.* It was a fudge-colored Rolls convertible. Very nice. "I may be well cared for," said Lucien.

"Cherished," I said. "Can you bark?"

The heat was dry and clean. We came blinking down the ladder. Dr. Bonni waited—penny loafers, checked pants, a cute blue blazer, soft red face with a dense Shell road map of exploded capillaries, hair dry and hand-tousled. "You must be . . ." he said.

"I am. And this is Lucien."

"Lucien," he breathed, "such a pretty name. I'm Gilbert and I always hated it. Gilbert," he said.

"Gilbert," Lucien repeated after him.

They were both staring at me. Somehow I had thought I would stay and describe the care and feeding of Lucien, or help him unpack, or maybe just bridge the gap between bride and bridegroom, but Dr. Bonni apparently only wanted me to disappear. Well, I couldn't turn around and climb back on the plane. "I guess I'll leave you two now," I said.

"Before I was a trainer, I was a vet," said Dr. Bonni.

"Veteran of what?"

"Veterinarian."

"Ah."

"So I can deliver health care if needed, or any other problems of adjustment. You may return whence you came."

He was in a hurry for something. He was the kind of distinguished lover who might hire an ambulance to meet his heart's desire at the airport, so that as the siren screamed and they sped home, he could perform his surgery on Palm Canyon Drive, on Lucien.

"You may tell the bishop, as I shall in due course, that you have completed your task. So go now," said Dr. Bonni.

He was holding Lucien's arm. There was a stiff grin on

Lucien's face which I had seen someplace before. On a boy who had lost his case for manslaughter by automobile—a difficult love matter and he backed over the girl in a driveway. On a black fragger, caught with grenades where he shouldn't have kept them. On my smiling dumb face when Priscilla said, Okay, that's enough, I think I'm grownup now, I want out.

I looked at where Dr. Bonni was holding the arm of Lucien and his claws with their clear polish were biting into Lucien's flesh. So that was why he showed the rigid death grin. And did he say nothing for the same reason I said nothing? Because we were determined, both of us, to go as far as we could with what we had started?

"It's time for you to be elsewhere in the world," said Dr. Bonni. "I'm sure you have many a task before you rest."

"I'm not sure."

Lucien was speaking very precisely. "Please. Stay till tomorrow, then come to take some letters to my family, come to say good-bye. Please. Please."

"It's not at all necessary," said Dr. Bonni. "I have stamps."

I looked at his tasseled shoes and then at his tasseled face with its meat striations in the cheeks and nose. "I have your address. I'll come tomorrow, Lucien," I said. "Now you two run along."

"We won't be home tomorrow," Dr. Bonni said. "You have no need. You are not invited."

"I'll be there."

The man smiled sweetly with his meat. His claws were still buried in Lucien's flesh and Lucien still wore that death grin. "The gate will be locked. You will be electrocuted if you try to climb through, and then perhaps you will be eaten by dogs. Truly, your work is done. Believe me. I have the word of the bishop about that. Please, Lucien, we have so much to do, we go now, my dear."

112

# 18

I heard what Dr. Bonni said, but I didn't listen to him.

Maybe I could just live through all this. Maybe it could just put the soundproof packing around my mutterings of loss. Maybe soon I'll go back to Poorman's Cottage in San Francisco to be a vegetarian, my feet firmly in the air, like a beet, but right now I'm still a flesh-eater. I want the wife I can't have. The meat I devour is my own.

It's an improvement as I lose feeling. I perch in the wind and say caw and cast cold black piercing crow looks at the world. I don't want to be bothered, but I still need carrion.

Didn't I hear this proverb in Haiti or Palm Springs, one of those places? You can't commit suicide without breaking eggs.

Shit! (Urban folk saying, U.S. of A.) I wasn't going to take any orders from any Dr. Gilbert Bonni. Could Lucien have had an idea of what part he would play in Dr. Bonni's dream? Maybe he thought he understood about the Worthingtons' play, and how for his role he would receive money, travel, a passage to the world of the North, and then he could come back to claim his Kenscoff sweetie and raise babies in a house with a concrete floor paid for by all the fun in Palm Springs. There was no way he could have known about Dr. Gilbert Bonni. For my own reasons, stupidity, not wanting to know, wanting very much to stupefy myself with strange, I hadn't thought it through either. To what I was delivering Lucien. To pain and shame and shit.

Second I would go look at the house. But first I had to bring a little healing emptiness of digestion into my life. I am not a light and easy vegetarian and I think evil thoughts and therefore I need my rest. While I rest and eat I think.

Scrambled eggs easy in the Baroque Bakery on Palm Canyon Drive, with a side order of all-meat patty, rare, plus seven-grain toast, plus Bottomless Cup of Coffee, followed by a nearly bottomless pee behind the door labeled *Tycoons*. (The other door was marked *Starlets*.)

While I rest and eat and pee, I sometimes try to think. The best I came to was that Lucien and I were bound together by ignorance and arrogance. We thought we could take care of ourselves by serving the Worthingtons. Neither of us knew and both of us had our reasons for not knowing what we were doing.

Now that I had an inkling, I just thought I'd hang around awhile. I had not brought all this trouble into my life just to end as a courier. Lucien was not a black bag of meat some bureaucrat had chained to my wrist. I didn't want to have as my last memory of him that death grin and the kindly veterinarian's clear-polished nails buried in his flesh.

I got directions. I walked past the twinkling colored lights, forever Christmas in the palm trees of Palm Canyon Drive, then turn right, then just beyond the wall.

Gilbert Bonni's cozy rancho on Ramon Drive is built in the shape of a piano, with the swimming pool nearby playing the part of kettle drum. A lovely ensemble seen from the air. Splish, splash, you could take a bath. From the ground, a white picket fence surrounds this little lounge orchestra, and behind the white picket fence a trench, and near the gate, behind the trench, two pretty layers of military barbed wire. The rest of the grounds is surrounded by a stone wall with jagged debris set into cement. Gilbert Bonni, animal chiropractor—he also advertises massage and hydro treatment for nervous pets—does not like to be disturbed unexpectedly. Perhaps he likes the expected disturbances. He must have purchased some of his gardening tools from the Alan Ladd Hardware Store, and he takes injured parties to the Dwight David Eisenhower Medical Center, and he likes to show visitors the Frank Sinatra Sculpture Court at the Desert Museum, and he rides his fudge-colored Rolls with the telephone and the air conditioning along Bob Hope Drive to the corner of Spiro T. Agnew Lane, where he has heart-to-heart talks. The fence around his property is a labor of love. By thinking about him, I made him less of a stranger. I would never get to be really his buddy.

Okay, now the wise scout retreats to organize. Perhaps Lucien might like living a few months or the rest of his life in a house shaped like a piano with a drum for bathing. Maybe he wouldn't mind about the wall with the broken bottles on top and the barbed wire and perhaps he didn't care if his life would be lazy. And, I was coming to believe, bloody.

In Poorman's Cottage I had grown accustomed to settling my lack of future by dreaming on it. Now I really needed to rest before I did anything hasty, brutal, and irrevocable. I asked for a room at the nearest hotel.

In fact, I needed an easy night away from Lucien in the Ingleside Inn. A fire blazed from oaken gas jets in the fireplace of the California Mission lobby and age forty-five starlets from L.A. and Chicago cackled and Steve McQueen failed to roar up on his motorcycle, as the resident manager remarked he did 'most every night when he was in town. Perhaps the explanation was simple—not in town. They did without rather than use Peter Fonda. The resident bartender whispered as he refilled my glass, "I think that's a live one over there." I looked over there and it looked like two live ones huddled together for comfort, both live, both in patched and faded French blue jeans penetrated by so many metal studs they should have shorted out the electrical equipment. They might be live, but I was worried and weary and not needing the comfort of these live ones. "They like to do together things," the bartender told me. "I advise you not to make a choice. I advise you to accept the goodies God brings you here on His desert."

I went to bed and found, in my unease, in this place, my jet lag, my loneliness, that I slept like a baby. Well, nothing is predictable. I thought of Dr. Bonni's claws buried in olive-dark skin, drawing little nicks of blood, but then I dreamt of nothing. Perhaps I don't remember my dreams anymore. I had had a few drinks.

And awoke with a start, unlike a baby, a sourness on my tongue, and busy dreading my meeting with Lucien and Gilbert Bonni. It was almost nine o'clock in the morning and I had managed to sleep through the sunrise and the jabber of skinny desert birds in the vines of my cabana. It seemed unnecessary to visit them one more time, just because Lucien imperatively asked me. Bishop Worthington had said, "Make the delivery and then go, don't wait, *go*. In addition to efficient arrivals, you are paid for rapid departures, also."

Why so uneasy here. This is a statement, not a question. I had a swim in the pool outside my door with its fallen palm leaves skating on the chlorinade. The sun and water were doing leather work to my skin. I wished I had a little squeeze bottle of lotion. Why so uneasy? This is now a question. Eggs again and bacon and coffee by the pool. If he made no sound when the claws bit his arm, why should I fail my duty to the Worthingtons?

If Lucien was satisfied, didn't that make it unanimous?

Did I envy how Lucien could make himself a new life?

And yet that face, like my own, smiling like death because it had no choice. And the voice, no resonance, carefully enunciating about letters to his village and good-bye to me. Maybe he really wanted to write letters home. Certainly he was frightened and wanted one last look at a face from his past. Funny that the last relic of Lucien's Haitian past was Sid Kasdan of Bernal Heights, San Francisco.

Someone had left an international airline squeeze bottle of lotion in the bathroom cabinet. My good luck. I squeezed. Milky sexy ooze to my flaking arms and nose.

Hell; do what I'm told, get this over with. I walked up Ramon Drive to the cozy rancho. My shoes crackled on desert rock. I rang the bell which said: *Tintinare.* There was no answer. I tried the picket fence gate. Locked. I had told Lucien I would visit him again and I would. I broke the catch with the kind of downward shove and jerk that gets a person a free newspaper from the coin dispenser. An insistent hum filled the air, then a tape of barking and snarling dogs. Stupid amateur security system. I kicked the speaker hidden in a dripping scarlet bougainvillea and the frantic barking snapped off. This was annoying anyway.

At the doorway in the garden stood a man in uniform, not a policeman, pointing what's that, a bayonet, at me. That's what it looked like—a very long knife, more like a slim garden tool, but very polished, a ritual gleam to it, and the man in uniform had the hooked cross symbol in patches on his arms and also on his knees. Goddamn swastikas on his knees, what did that mean? Gilbert Bonni was threatening to eviscerate me.

"Oh help! Oh help!" Lucien was on the floor behind him, bleeding thin spleeny blood, with tiny patterned shal-

117

low scratches—like an allergy test—over his naked upper body, chest and arms and bleeding nipples. "Get out!" said the good Dr. Bonni.

"What the devil is going on?"

"First of all, you were supposed never to be seen again. Second, you have no right to force your way into my house."

"If you hurt me it is only self-defense, right?" I asked.

He advanced. "I would like that."

Lucien crossed his arms over his chest to hide his wounds. It was a girlish gesture of modesty.

"But don't hurt me," I told the good doctor. "It would be inconvenient."

"The bishop said you were reliable, you piece of pork."

I checked the position of the long knife (upraised for threatening, not underhanded for evisceration), the marbled capillaries of his nose and chins, the nice shiny cloth with its satiny swastika decals in out-of-the-way places. I would take a chance on outgassing him. "For fucking Nazi drag your vocabulary is all wrong, Gilbert."

He cocked his head to try to make sense of that mouthful. It bothered him and the knife started to slide down toward the evisceration position, where it could do harm to my digestion. I wondered if he was a GP veterinarian or a specialist in canine allergies. I kept an eye on him and said, "Lucien, are you hurt?"

And Lucien said an astonishing thing. "No. Thank you very much. He is very kind to give me stamps."

"You don't want to be taken away?"

"Merci bien, non. I will mail my letters. I will stay here with my friend."

"What the shit kind of doctor are you?" I asked Bonni.

"Get out. Get out. Get out. You are meddling. Get out," he said, "and you may yet save your life, Jew."

Lucien smiled like a submissive wife.

I thought of my options. The police. Violence here and now. Few others except a walk back down the quiet road to my hotel. I was walking back down the quiet desert road without a good-bye from Lucien.

If it didn't hurt, why did he beg for help? If it hurt, why did he smile and tell me to go? Again I was making my old mistake of trying to understand others. Again I was making my old mistake of trying to understand myself.

On all sides some kind of desert toad was croaking under the starlight. I had scampered when the vet told me to. Lucien too. It was bad enough to get confused signals from others. It was worse to send them to myself.

Some of those toads, I could see from the leathery relics on the road, took time out from croaking to scamper unsuccessfully under passing cars. They never knew whether it was a Cadillac Seville or a Toyota pickup that transformed them.

Worse than a mistake is a misstep. I was not sure how the misstep I had made this morning would affect my future with the Worthington enterprises. I had little knowledge of them, either. A good Jewish survivor should really make better plans than I do. What I still planned to do was to follow the plans of others, even when, like Lucien, they decided their plans on insufficient evidence from moment to moment, or like Dr. Bonni and the Worthingtons, they wanted for me only what they needed for themselves.

Next time I visited the desert I must bring a decent lotion. At my age, the skin freckles and gets liver spots, not that nice rosy tan Priscilla picks up if she just peeks through the window on a day of swift sunlight.

At Kennedy, when I emerged into the tunnels which lead to someplace else, a mole burrowing, carrying my bag and headed for baggage, feeling my peeling tan, my skin

119

yellowed by sun, travel, and anxiety, wondering how they blew air over the other preoccupied moles, expecting to get in touch with someone . . . they got in touch with me. They didn't wait. At baggage, Luci, whom I had wanted to call stranger, stood smiling and tapping a little half-heel, letting the traffic eddy about her, like a cute greeter—a secretary or a light of love. She leaned up to kiss me, raising one foot. There was no sex in this kiss; why should there be?

"Hi, Sid, have a good trip?"

"Hi, stranger."

"Oh, Sid. But I'm really real, you know."

Well, why shouldn't there be some juice in this greeting? Last time I saw her, there was juice in the farewell. She was neat and crisp and pretty and smelled of a light commercial cologne. She was in full Manhattan lower-middle career girl drag.

"Been a busy time, Luci."

"And we sure want to talk about that, Sid."

So we had company. Out of the crowd came several loiterers who had been watching this connection. They looked like the negatives of customs agents or FBI men. They wore hats, trenchcoats, and thin slashes of mouth, two stalwart chaps. They intended to monitor the discussion. The light in that tunnel was, oh, tirelessly flickering, fluorescent. I was a student of life, but the course seemed too difficult.

As I took note of these old-fashioned haberdashery enthusiasts, Luci kissed me again, in a busy way, and whispered sweet nothings to me: Please come with me now are you really alone to the conference room we have rented only to talk with you my dear friend and colleague. You *are* alone, aren't you, Sid?

Their Ford was safely parked in a red zone. They got in on both sides of me and Luci drove. They led me into a double room at the Airport Hilton. They let me carry my

120

own luggage. I had been in that hotel before, but this time was different. I remembered when Luci had played mute. Now she was playing talker. "Be patient, just rest back," she said. "I plan to run this session."

"I don't like it."

"You look worried."

"I am worried."

She touched my shoulder and winked. "Okay, I like you, I like you, I like you. Now you feel better?"

"Not very much."

"Well, I'll say one thing for you. You're not susceptible to flattery. And you've got a strong streak of realism in your character even if you tend to, oh, think your own thoughts. That's two or three things, I guess. I *want* you to be worried, Sid."

"I don't think you like me."

"I don't dislike you."

"That's not the same thing in my system. You'd hurt me if it suited you."

She grinned like a flirty girl. "Only physically. Your mental and emotional state interests you, though, too much for a man in your position, Sid."

I wanted to keep her talking. It felt safer. It felt as if I had a measure of control over her actions if she kept talking. "My health interests me also," I said, "good health and an exciting old age."

"The macho character of a born failure, my friend. Why don't you just do as you're told?"

I shrugged. A shrug means one wants to interdict the weight, let it slide off the back. I too am a creature of my history. The two negative customs men had walked on either side of us, jostling travelers, in formation not to be interrupted by mere courtesy or comfort. They didn't mind greasing their haberdashery with human contact. They thought I might run, and that made me want to run.

The room was Hilton Airport Imperial—wood that was not wood and paintings that were not paintings and a color TV that was a real color TV. For some reason it irritated me that the TV had been left on and a daytime game show was playing to the unoccupied room when we entered. One of the haberdashery models turned it on its swivel to the wall but did not turn it off. The television mutter of greed, laughter, and applause rumbled beneath our negotiations. I remembered when I thought Luci mute. Funny games she played. But now I liked her better that other way.

She turned her pretty head toward the bathroom door, and as if on signal, I heard the plumbing work. What toilet flushes when a crisp little slave trader looks in its direction? Answer: the commode flushed by—the door opened—Jan Worthington followed by his brother, the bishop.

"Shit," I said.

"Very sweet," said the bishop, "in this temporal world of woe we waste too much time in idle chatter."

"Luci," I said. Reproach just leaked out of me.

"I'm changeable," said Luci. Her eyes were blinking. Apparently she was adjusting to new contact lenses. "I'm not reliable. I'm not perfect. I'm sorry."

"What's happening?" I asked. Nobody answered. "Okay, where're Father Brice and Mahmoud? Shouldn't we have a party?"

The Worthingtons looked at each other and Luci looked at me. "Died," she said. "Sad case. Turned out worse than you, Sid, and so he passed on. It doesn't pay to be as bad as you, much less worse, Sid."

I tried to remember Mahmoud in my cottage in San Francisco, where just now the junk mail was piling up behind the door and there were no personal letters at all waiting to be answered. At first Mahmoud seemed to run things, but he didn't. If they had killed him, they were foolish to let me know. Unless they were not foolish, and they didn't seem to be, in which case it was a serious threat about my life, in case I cared. Which meant I might not get back to the cottage where Mahmoud had dealt into my willing hands the beginning of his (their) plan. And the mail would be stamped *Return to Sender* if they do that with junk mail. And my wife might have a twinge of regret along with the twinges of satisfaction, a nice warm glow because no fleshly ghost would come bothering her at some inconvenient moment in her future or present happiness.

I wondered if Luci gave Mahmoud a sexing good-bye before she dispatched him. She seemed to like putting the seal of her body on the events of financial and power accumulations.

There was a soft scratching at the door. It was not a bell-man's or a maid's sound. Jan opened and a soft, fat voice complained, "I went to the wrong room, not the right one." It was a very fat man in wide-wale purple corduroys to make the most of his bulk. I had met him before. "Bon jour, Mahmoud," I said.

"Paris," he said, "San Francisco. How good of you to remember."

"You've gained a lot of weight."

"Glands. I've got greasy glands, plus eating too much, Meester Sid."

"Where's Magda?" I asked him.

She was hidden behind him. When they shut the door, she removed her pistol and began snapping things into it, cleaning and adjusting. The feeling was not that of a trial anymore. It was that of an execution squad. But how had I merited so grand an occasion? I turned to the bishop. "I thought you told me he died."

"That's a mere detail, my dear. Luci meant the unfortunate Father Brice. The rest you supplied."

"Another thing about you, Sid," Luci said, "is you have a slight case of runaway mouth."

"You were troubled about poor Mahmoud here. That's lovely of you. You like to take care of people where it's no proper duty of yours." The bishop was smiling a bit and unsticking his lips. There was amusement and satisfaction and maybe even a certain appetite in the gesture of saliva coming undone between tongue and mouth. And yet his pleasure gave me no joy.

"What could Brice have done to you?" I asked.

"He could have done so much, but he didn't do it right," said Luci.

"He was our brother," said Jan.

"Requiescat in pace," said the bishop.

"Bad blood, you understand, is worse in families than between friends," Jan said.

"Evidently you don't have any enemies," I said. "You just have friends and relatives to kill."

"Oh no, who said that?" Mahmoud asked. He loosened his belt, which was partly capped by a large silver buckle with twin gladiators striving on it. Either he was gaining ounces this very moment or my miniature grief about the Haitian priest had made him flatulent.

Magda smiled at me. "It is much better to be an associate and to enjoy enduring common interests, is it not?"

The Worthingtons nodded. Luci looked bored. Mahmoud, sweating, for some additional reason was annoyed with Magda. Perhaps he remembered that she and I . . . I remembered it, too, and even recalled my pleasure despite this occasion in which doubt and anxiety should have occupied all my attention. The advantage of a very unhappy end of marriage is that afterward you don't worry too much about survival. Not being a drinker or a fast driver, I took different chances with my body.

This was a nice big family we had here.

The Worthingtons looked smily and unperturbed in their light linen suits, white in color, setting off the seamed

middle-aged tans of light-skinned folks permanently de-
tailed to the tropics. The bishop wore a white turtleneck
with a scarlet clerical collar. "Bless his soul, he didn't have
much family feeling," he said, and I realized he was reply-
ing to my spoken and unspoken thoughts about Father
Brice.

"You did okay in Frankfurt, Sid," Jan said. "The test delivery went fine—"

"For that was what it was, a type of test," said
Mahmoud.

"We had excellent hopes for you, Sid," Luci said. "Personally, I enjoyed you."

Jan Worthington kept switching on and off a flamelet of
smile, like a Cricket cigarette lighter.

There was another knock at the door and Jan simply
opened it as if he knew whom to expect. It was my friend,
the deeply southern stew. She smiled her coffee-tea-or-
milk, raised-in-Atlanta smile at me—yes, I know you and I
remember—and then moved to Luci, who put her arm
around her. They kissed on the lips. It was unnecessary to
discipline me in this peculiar way, I thought.

Mahmoud said, "I think I have to hurt you."

"I'm sure that isn't necessary," I said.

"Are you insulting my honor?"

"No, of course not. I hate fist-fighting."

"You do not choose to dirty yourself with me? You are
in some way better than an Arab?"

"Don't be silly."

"Now you are calling me stupid!"

He was whipping himself stolidly into a rage. Was there
any way to divert the plan? "I apologize," I said.

"So you admit you called me stupid! Smart Yid!"

No way to get out of it. I felt a sigh coming up from deep
within. Mahmoud's little fat eyes were red-rimmed. Whatever the plan, his rage was now genuine. I looked at Luci

and my stewardess, both of whom had enjoyed ... No, I had enjoyed good sex, fairly good sex with both of them. Would it please them now to see me killed? Or merely badly hurt?

They were enfolded in each other's arms and kissing, and they began to make their kind of love as Mahmoud, while the Worthingtons held me, began methodically to punch my arms and legs, catching nerves I didn't know I had, a sizzle going up and down my spine, a blow to my arm which made my fingertips explode, me observing this, Sid observing this, until I fainted from the pain.

The Worthingtons lifted me back to my feet. Someone slapped my cheek sharply twice. I was awake. I had not fouled my pants yet. By this time in my life I knew enough to trust nobody but myself, but could my own body be trusted? My mind had already drifted elsewhere. I still felt something, a bit of fear. I still felt in their distant places my old losses. I still remembered these recent weeks hurtling about the globe. I had taken deep note of how Lucien seemed not to mind being cut and cut and cut. He knew his lover would not kill him. Or perhaps he didn't know it.

I was feeling something else which I chose not to name.

Mahmoud was smiling and hot and grunting. He would lose weight at this pace.

Blessedly, the pain seemed to come to me from afar, and so did my words, "Stop, oh stop," so that I must have felt them. Darkness then.

# Part II

*My mother and father died before the age I have reached now. I've not had any children yet and maybe never will. It looks that way. If my mother had decided she wanted freedom from her husband and marriage, as my wife did, it might have been easier on my father. My father was dead at forty.*

*But I don't know. Priscilla wasn't easy on me.*

*I stopped smoking, I watch my weight, exercise. I'm healthy. I have a toe missing, left a stub in Korea. It only hurts when I walk too much with rapid turns. The disability of a headquarters company interrogator who can now never become a classical ballerina. Well, eight percent disability pay keeps me in books, magazines, and movies. I can go to the V.A. hospital for cheap vitamins. As a private investigator, I took buses and left the car for my wife. I never meet a woman who notices my missing toe until I point to it and tell her how lucky I was to catch the slightest edge of the mine. "What's that there?" Priscilla asked with her nose slightly wrinkled. "It's not there," I said. "Oh dear," she said. "Say 'Hero,'" I said. But she couldn't quite squeeze out the word. Nobody can. They're right not to.*

*When I was a boy, I thought I had elephant ears. Then I got used to it. Only jug ears. "The better to steer you by," my wife used to say when she felt jolly. "Say 'sahib,'" I said. But she seldom felt that jolly.*

*Nevertheless, early on, she wanted a child. I didn't; I wanted her love first. Then I wanted a child and she didn't. I really wanted it then. And she really, really, really wouldn't. "Getting together" doesn't mean people have gotten together.*

*I gave up smoking eleven years ago. The first time I met her, she told me my breath smelled like an ashtray. I never wanted a smoke again after I started wanting her. Oh, a cigar on national holidays when she bought me one, or a gift from a proud new father; I smoked them for sharing and for good luck. Now that she's left me, I sometimes wake up with that ashtray taste on my tongue, but I still don't smoke. You never know whom you'll meet around the next corner.*

*My grandmother lived forever. When I last saw her, she was tied to a chair, with a sheet. She asked me, "Which doctor are you?" "I'm not a doctor," I said. She said, "Well, I don't talk to no orderlies, mister."*

*I couldn't remember—I had buddies then!—like my grannie I couldn't remember a single name of my buddies in the 88th, Seoul North, heading north a little and getting killed; not heading north too much. I was in headquarters*

128

*company because I was so gifted in the head. I didn't use it too much there, either.*

*I can't remember the names of those buddies, but I remember I loved them. My wife can't remember when she loved me, but I'll bet she still remembers my name. Only she can't remember why.*

*The first girl I ever went to bed with broke into tears; it was her first time, too. It wasn't "to bed with," that's just an expression; it was to back seat of Rambler with. I didn't burst into tears. I asked her why so much emotion and she said, "I wanted you to make it beautiful." "For us both?" I asked her. Maybe I would know enough to cry the last time I go to back seat with a woman.*

*It's foolish of men to love dead women, it's foolish of women to love dead men, and yet they do. It's foolish of me to love a departed woman. At least with a dead person, one can embrace memories. Sensible Priscilla tried to take care of this option before she left me. And yet I clung to someone cozy and welcoming, long after she became none of this to me. Her eyelashes used to flutter, tickling, against my cheeks as we slept—what the devil did we do with our noses? We woke up and laughed. Sneaky! How did you get that in when I wasn't looking? And I answered, You were looking, only you were asleep. And she said, That's not a mere detail, sneaky thing. Goodnight again. And I said, I can't do this all by myself. And she said, Well, I'm closing down now, back to dreamytime—and a wild look of laughter in her eye before she shut it and began breathing slowly, slowly, slowly, faster.*

*"Good goddamn but you're lucky beyond what you deserve," she said when we both finished. She never gave me credit for any of her own good luck. But anyway I used to sleep in peace.*

*Not sleeping in peace anymore, I am beginning to limp forward into older age. Good-bye to Poorman's Cottage, welcome to Turmoil Village, now located in the Airport Hilton.*

**19** When I awoke in the darkened room, I was alone. I was not alone. Luci was sitting by my side, stroking my arm. She had put some sort of cooling substance on the swellings. It was evaporating fast with an invisible vapor. It stung. I sat up. That was a clever bruiser. I was especially sore in the shoulders, but I could move okay. I must have been out only a few minutes. The shades were drawn in the pseudo-night of luxurious hotel rooms, and the group was gone, except for Luci. I was groggy. There was a plane taking off, thin whine, nearby. I said, "So I didn't behave as you expected. Why didn't you kill me?"

"Some thought that would be a desirable solution. Personally, I like you."

"Thanks a lot."

"I argued for a lesson, and then I volunteered to talk with you to make sure we understand each other."

"There is no failure of communication. It's what we communicate that makes difficulties."

"You don't seem to be working out, Sid."

"And now?"

"We want you to find another means to express yourself.

131

We want you to forget you ever met us. I'm even giving you a little money, if you look in your pants pocket, it's in hundred-dollar bills, real ones, no works of art, so you won't have any consumer complaints. We don't want to kill you. Or maybe we do, but I personally do not."

"I sure appreciate that."

"I didn't *like* Father Brice, he lacked panache."

"A capital offense, Luci."

"Never mind."

I considered whether I had enough panache to save my life. "You want me to do what?" I asked.

"It doesn't hurt us about Father Brice, since we're not a very sentimental family."

"Are you sentimental about me?"

"We're in the business of *selling* occasions for feeling, Sid. We don't buy them. We treat the sick without necessarily treasuring their disease. But you're funny, I always thought. So gray and bruised. And yet so . . . oh, normally words come easy to me . . . volatile. I think that's the word which should come easy to me as I search my vocabulary. Yes, that's probably it, Sid. Yes, you're okay."

"Does that mean I'm safe? Father Brice wasn't."

"No. And he tracked you, found you, did a little analysis, picked you, too. He had his points, even if they weren't always good points. But now he serves once more—to get through to your, oh, volatility, Sid, that it's time to behave yourself. To be strict with yourself, not volatile. We really and truly and earnestly and with no volatility at all mean that. We don't like to make trouble for the Worthingtons, and killing is never convenient, but if letting you bump around makes embarrassment for my brothers and me—"

"So what should I do?"

"I'm so glad you inquired. Go back to San Francisco and lead an average upset private eye's average little life, Sid." She stood up and went to the door. She lingered. "You know what?" She positively hung back. "In some ways I'm deeply disappointed in you. But speaking personally, I'd like one more . . ."

"You're mega-crazy," I said.

She opened the door and was gone. There were fifty one-hundred-dollar bills in my pocket. They would look at me twice with my bruises and my faded yellow tan when I tried to change them, but I could handle that. I was thinking about what I had just said. Crazy. Crazy. I might be volatile, but they were insane and I had brought Lucien to a man who would torture him, might murder him for the fun and panache of it, and they had paid me for this service.

How unwell they knew me. Now I had ready cash for the cash-thirsty moments ahead.

The pig never looks at the sky; that's why it's said to be wise. But it's only wiser than dogs and cats, and soon it turns into pork. I wanted to see that patch of blue and brilliance, that yellow sun, that wan gray glow of San Francisco in the afternoon. I wanted to turn my face to the sky and not be pork. I was homesick. Yet I hadn't enjoyed my last year at home. So I was not ready to go back yet. Since the Worthingtons wanted me home, I wanted first of all to finish what I had started.

A few hours later I was on a flight filled with very well-off real estate developers, legal and medical practitioners, and stars of stage, screen, television, and widowhood. The village of Palm Springs merited nonstop jet service from New York. Did Luci and the Worthingtons think I wouldn't take this trip if they volunteered insults instead of murder?

The sun shined on. I didn't look at the sky.

Best to rent a car at the traditional chrome-and-glass stage near the Palm Springs Convention and Visitors Bureau. If you don't have credit cards (I had let mine expire), they will take cash after some earnest persuasion. I was studying social graces; life enforced careful attention to the direct look, the ingratiating smile, the pocket full of money. The pink-haired desert Hertz lady looked at my money as if a rare desert lizard had been dropped by the tail on her counter. It was dead. Why didn't I take that stuff to Budget or Avis? She picked it up by the ears, put it in a drawer, and said, "Normally we don't. But since you're willing to leave a thousand-dollar cash deposit—"

"I'm not eager. I have no choice."

"In your case, we'll make an exception."

"Thank you very much. Now one two three, let's both smile for the risk we're taking."

Under that hair which stood up like some absolutely Now television reception device, her eyes and mouth, together, in unison, did not smile. I shut up. I had the keys, but I didn't yet have the car. "Stall 5," she said. "Map and instructions on the seat. Please note your mileage."

I thought it best to wait until dusk, which comes sooner than elsewhere, the sun signing out early behind its implacable guard of mountains. The San Jacinto range stands naked, spines of purple and gray rock shifting in the light with their lunar changes. I sat outdoors—rash of me—at an espresso place on Palm Canyon Drive, admiring the hobbled walks of the ladies riding on top of their cork soles, and the no-hip skinnies from Beverly Hills, and the non-skinnies leaving mascara like bird droppings on the sidewalk every time they blinked. Probably a fellow could learn to relax in a town like this. I wasn't there first with the thought.

Finally the blue haze of evening and it was time. I penetrated the luxury car parade toward the ends of town, past Liberace's piano-shaped house, past the down-home mansion of a country-western star with its Nashville Greek columns, past the houses of many anonymous, retired, but still practicing millionaires—a tennis ball sailed up and out into the street from a sunken tennis court—and there was our friend the veterinarian tycoon's white-walled rancho. I parked. I thought to wait till it was completely dark.

Glimpses and glimmers of lights through the fence told me people were moving about. Perfect, of course, would be for Dr. Bonni to go out on an errand and leave Lucien behind. Then I would have only fences, walls, alarms, dogs, guards, and mechanical contrivances to obstruct me. No such luck. No one emerged. A Mexican boy on a three-wheeled vehicle delivered flowers, then left. That was all.

So despite his garden, nice sadistic Dr. Bonni liked fresh flowers brought to the house.

In the dark I moved to the gate. I didn't enjoy all these burglar facilities. I edged along the short double fence of barbed wire to the wall and examined it. There were little crevices where my shoes might hold. Perhaps I could climb okay (the missing toe ached already); but on top of the stone there were broken bottles, jagged spikes set in cement, a row of glass and metal incisors stretched around the house like a gigantic set of brontosaurus teeth. Possibly if a fellow had a couple of thick blankets or sleeping bags to throw over the wall . . . no.

I returned to the gate and rang the bell. A soft voice finally answered. "Who is it?"

"Flower boy."

"We got the flowers already. Gladiolas."

"Meester, farm-fresh roses, my boss say, ees geeft for you."

Of course he could have had a TV monitor. The buzzer sounded. I entered. I walked through a narrow cactus garden distributed among a collection of desert rocks. Lizards played in the dark like mice.

I didn't have to open the kitchen door. It was open. I entered. Dr. Bonni slouched comfortably in a kitchen chair with a hunting rifle propped in his crotch, but pointed at my crotch. The shot which would kill me would castrate him. He should move it before he used it.

"That thingee's not safe like that," I said.

His mouth spread in a Gilbert Bonni smile. "Different strokes for different folks. What the fuck you doing back here?"

"Lonely for Lucien."

He understood that. He kept the rifle in his crotch, where he probably wouldn't use it, but he didn't leap up to offer me a glass of milk from the fridge. He understood, but he didn't believe. "You finished your job."

"I'd like to see him."

"That's nice. Perhaps I might even like you to see him. I'm so proud of his progress. But he particularly left instructions he didn't like to see you. Right now he's having his bath followed by his beauty rest. We're having company later."

"I don't believe part of that."

"He bathes. He sleeps."

"He likes to see me, Gilbert."

"Dr. Bonni. If you had a sick pet turkey, you would talk different to me, mister. When people need me, they are respectful."

"Dr. Bonni, I want to talk with Lucien."

"Mr. Sid," he said, "I'm afraid you can't."

"I'll wait."

"I advise not waiting here. I advise shuffling off elsewhere to entertain yourself before you take the first flight out in the morning. I happen to know a lovely, energetic dog groomer—a gay lady, of course— who could teach you a few tricks, Mr. Sid. She'll comb the lice out of your fur, for example."

"I'm afraid my dance card is filled."

"For a man with a rifle pointed at his balls, your tongue is kind of loose."

"You don't want to shoot."

"Oh no. You're wrong about that. I do very much want to shoot. My own best interests, however, are served by getting you the fuck out of here—*now!*" He stood up and despite the wobble of his belly had a way of briskly lifting the rifle to his shoulder. He pointed it briefly to the door through which I had come and then lowered it again. It would make a loud dirty noise as the shell ripped through my skull. But Lucien appeared behind him, saying, "It will be the end if you do that, uncle."

"I'll do it!" he shrieked.

"When you lose your temper," Lucien said, "I do not like it." But then he said to me, very rapidly, "Often he loses his temper. Please."

I had a clue about Bonni, however. He was lonely and bored. I understood that. "Can we just talk a few minutes first?" I asked. "I know you'd like some target practice on me, but it would be so messy—"

"I'll have you stuffed for my playroom!"

"Uncle," said Lucien. Lucien took him seriously.

"Just a little conversation," I said out there in the Palm Springs desert country where this pear-shaped single swinger stood cautiously waving his rifle from me to Lucien and then back to me. Somebody would get killed if everybody wasn't careful. Although the rashness of my eighteenth year was long gone, those years when I was sure of my immortality, I lacked the caution proper to my time in life. Grief, loneliness, and the need for distraction tend to bring back the style of adolescence in those whose bodies manage to hold up. I was having a night session in front of a rifle. "Please move that ugly thing," I said.

"Talk," he said. "You have a two-minute meter running. After that I don't accept explanations."

"You make it hard to banter, fella," I said.

He shrugged and pointed the muzzle at me. "There's not

137

much you can do and nothing you can do about what you can't do."

"I can't even get what I want."

Bonni looked sad. "Sometimes you can't even get what you don't want. I find that's a fact. I even forget what I want sometimes, and consequently it gives me special pleasure to have it all clear in my mind just now. If you jump, I shoot."

"You play endgame, doctor. It doesn't make for good sport."

"Please explain, I speak English, but explain," said Lucien.

Bonni ignored his words while emitting a long lingering languorous gaze at his person. He sighed. "Sid," he then asked me, "is your own life serious to you, or is it just something you do? I know your *attitudes* are serious to you, but is that enough?"

"Probably not."

"So then something else should be."

"I doubt you've been in love. I have been." I am, I thought. This was a family-size psychopath, despite his cute Palm Springs rancho. Why was I talking to him as if he were a reasonable business psychopath, like the Worthington twins?

"What's that croaking outside, Dr. Bonni? Crickets?" I asked.

"Desert toads. Can't you tell? It's a dirtier sound. They come into my garden and eat the poison and just get fat. I really think they get fat on the hydroxycoumarin."

"Lots of us get fat on poison, doctor. Don't!" I said suddenly. Bonni whirled the rifle toward Lucien, then back to me. It was an ungainly weapon for close quarters. It could smash up a custom rancho kitchen and us beyond any handyman's ability to fix. "Okay," I said, "I wanted to see if you would shoot or play Ping-Pong."

"I might have."

138

"You don't want to do all that damage."

He was sighting down the barrel. "If I have to."

"You don't want to kill us."

"You. Not Lucien."

I tried not moving and not speaking a moment to quiet him. He too was volatile. Toadsong filled the house. My ears had gotten acute; probably Dr. Bonni's, also. I wanted to give him time to consider. To hear the world around him. To remember, as I occasionally tried to, that there could be another future than the one he was sliding into.

Moving very slowly is the only way with a volatile fat one like that, stuffed with poison as he was. Okay. Now I'll move. I said, "Come on, Lucien."

Lucien understood. He stepped in front of the rifle, and I held him from behind. (Arrested for following too closely—the old joke ran through my head.) We lock-stepped toward the door.

There were tears on Bonni's cheeks. "I might! I might!"

"Please don't," I said.

At the door we paused for a moment, not for any senti-mental good-byes to the weeping lover we were leaving behind, but simply to work the latch. Bonni was broken-hearted. He put down the weapon. He didn't want to hurt Lucien. He said softly through his sobs, "They'll find you, they'll kill you."

"Thank you very much."

"Oh my dear, my dear. If it takes days, weeks, months, they will."

"I have the time. Good-bye."

We were in the thin evening chill of the desert outside, bougainvillea smells from the garden and chlorine from the pool. "You are peculiar," said Lucien.

"Get in the car quick," I said. "So are you. You made a deal and you didn't stick to it."

"So did you," he said.

**20** We sat awhile in silence as I drove down to Palm Canyon Drive and then out of the village, keeping exactly five miles above legal speed through the desert toward the next village and the next one, date plantations, motels, retirement compounds, a trailer park billed as Rolling Condos. I had a plan. I would have liked to make this transfer by solid-state technology, the transmigration of bodies, but didn't own the equipment yet. A desert junker would have to do. I wanted just to leave the rent-a-car to be found someplace, preferably nearby.

"Is money their life?" Lucien asked me.

"Money is not their life."

The tumbleweed and the skeletal desert vegetation moved in night winds. Suddenly, although it was still early, the world was empty. A full moon in clear skies. Along with the empty world, I was thinking: No jokes. They'll kill.

"Is sex, their kind of sex, their life?"

"Sex is certainly not their life," I said.

I had a plan. I wanted to get to Twenty-Seven Palms before ten o'clock. I had a reason for this; and I had better be correct in my reason, and correct in my reasons to come, if I were to undo the harm I had already done. I wanted both Lucien and me to cut free. This complicated thing had to be done right.

In the middle of the village stood a large packed lot with lightbulbs bright and burning and the sign:

GOOD TRANSPORTATION

A salesman was lounging in the shack (All-Nite Ace on Duty), waiting for someone in the market for reliable movement. That described me perfectly. "I got a nice Camaro here, steel-belt radials, you might think it was drove by a crazed rice-eating hot-rodder and we set back the speedometer, but I swear the Chinese was a backyard futzer and he set back the speedometer hisself haha . . . We retail here at wholesale rates, 'cause people just drop in the desert, you know . . ."

"Something cheaper but it runs," I said.

The soaped windshields said: 2 Dentist-Owner . . . Chicago Special, No Salt . . . $1299 Till Dawn . . . 4-Speaker Stereo, Fun Wheels Never Been to Mexico . . . No talk of cam shafts and transmissions in this marketplace. It was an encouraging code if you knew what it meant and you were speaking to All-Nite Ace of Twenty-Seven Palms.

"How about a sixty-six Caddy, air condish, all-automatic windows, lousy gas, sweet-looker, really à la carte, you're a prince of the road—it was drove by this chiropodist hardly drove it, had his office in one wing of his El Spanish Mission ranchito—"

"Maybe someday I'll be in the market, but I want something less—"

"*Less?*" He was shocked. I looked like a nicer person. "Less à la carte?"

"Just less." I spotted an old Ford convertible with a

muddy white top and edges eaten out by eastern snow-removal salt. Chalked on the window was its epitaph:

RUNS GOOD MAKE OFFER

I decided to make offer. "Six bills right now to drive it away if I drive it once around the block and it's table d'hôte—transmish doesn't die on me."

"Seven," he said. "Plus minimum paperwork. Cash bucks. Are you dealing?"

"Dealing," I said.

"I don't think the mufflers'll go on you?" he asked as if this were the question of the week. He darted an Ace of a glance at Lucien, who thought he understood English but didn't understand our voodoo negotiations. "Your friend knows what he wants. You just put those mufflers up with the Dentyne gum in the holes and the Scotch Tape if they start to go on you. But you rather ride in a Caddy, hey boy?"

Lucien smiled and looked away. Lucien didn't know what I wanted. I didn't know. But this shrewd dealer in his snap-buttoned Western shirt knew that I wanted something.

The Ford was about twelve years old and maybe a kid would have paid four hundred for it. The body was shot. But I saw the tires were okay. It would give speed if I needed it. V-8 engine. The radio worked. We had a long trip across America to endure together, Lucien and the Ford and I. Ace and I took a ride around the lot, leaving Lucien to browse among the zoo of cars. The Ford bent around corners; the frame wobbled a little. The motor was solid, and getting us someplace fast was what I wanted to do. And somehow I liked the idea of the ragtop down, taking the sun, breathing the air of Arizona and Texas and Louisiana and Florida, maybe doing side roads just in case.

On the side roads, the ragtop would pay us back in ease.

"I'll buy it," I said, "if you can do your minimum paperwork in about ten minutes."

"Our operation is set up for that," Ace said cheerfully, "we got the equipment for it. You ain't planning to drive over to Mexico, are you? I mean, if you're a mule—shit, ain't my responsibility."

"No, I'm not."

"Because this is reliable transportation, but it—"

"I'm in a hurry."

"—*looks* unreliable, and the federales—" So you can't tell about people. Ace really did have my interests at heart. Those bitten nails with destroyed stubs of fingertips came from worrying about others.

"I appreciate your interest and concern, friend. Now can your back office get to the papers?"

"Rot cheer I'm the back office, friend. Minimum's the word. But you ain't got no claim in such a hurry, 'cause your little buddy there he done wandered off."

Lucien! The dark sparkly desert night around the rows of electric bulbs was empty. He was gone. Medium-sized, big-hearted Ace was smiling and pointing a finger: that way. I ran. I didn't even ask if something had driven up and taken him off. What a stupid thing, to drive around the lot without him. Stupid, stupid, stupid, and why was Ace grinning?

Down the street, the one paved street I suspected (wrong about that), a dark figure was pressed against the glass of a closed drugstore. He didn't see me come up. Lucien was peering into the blackness, studying something within. "What is it, why'd you go without telling me, what are you looking at?"

"This shop is closed," Lucien said poignantly.

"Everything is closed down. I bought a Ford. What are you doing here?"

143

"I need . . . I need a transistor to take home with me, and look, they have batteries and the case and everything. At what time do they open the shop?"

I grabbed him and said, "We've got to hurry. Look, friend. Someplace along the line they are hunting for us. We can't wait around, our best shot is hurrying quietly, Lucien."

Stricken deep disappointment on his face.

"But I suspect there'll be another drugstore, maybe a radio shop, you'll be able to buy what you need. Come on now. Come on."

He followed lightly, limberly, as I trotted back to the Christmas tree brightness of the car orchard where desert transportation thrived in an oasis of friendly greed. Ace just said, "Sign here and she's yours. Nice adequate wheels without excess cheerismo."

He kicked the tires good-bye. A sentimental person. "Bye-bye, come back our way soon and say hello."

We headed south and east, and I noticed too late that the car pulled to the right. Well, a little bent frame never hurt anyone. The tires would wear a bit faster. They should last until Miami, though, wouldn't they? And then, when Lucien was home in Kenscoff again, I could go back to San Francisco like a normal person, and find a woman with a master's degree in Batik, a minor in Macramé, and we could retreat to the country together to raise low-cal honey from bees doing their job of pollination on astroturf. Amen. Lucien rested his chin on his fist and his eyes blinking sleepily, telephone pole, telephone pole, telephone pole, the rhythm putting him to sleep. In a different way from me, he didn't care what happened to him.

The Hertz people would pick up their car. Ace wouldn't know where I was going—probably Mexico. The Worthingtons needed a little confusion in their lives.

We drove through southern California until two in the

morning, through that air of a dry dungeon, cooked every day, hung out all night, until the fatigue hit me like a dead mattress sailing through alley air. Country-western music could not keep me awake. I was ready to drop in a corner and sink. Perhaps I would find some speed from your friendly small-town pharmacist later in this trip, but now I just wanted to sleep, I had to sleep, and I thought the Worthingtons would keep busy checking airports if they checked anything at all, and we might as well disappear for a few hours. I stopped at a motel that said, *Six Dollar Motel Six* (*Rooms Now Sixteen Dollars*). Lucien looked at me with a little smile, and I thought he wanted to ask about the price of the room, and then I understood what he was asking.

"No, not necessary," I said.

"If you wish," he said.

"I don't wish. I'm just tired of driving."

"If only I could drive," he said, "I could help you drive. But I can relax."

"Then relax."

"You," he said. "You need. Nobody will know. I tell nobody."

"No. Thanks. No."

He shrugged and turned away. He was sure I was wrong. He was sure I would change my mind. He was sure I was afraid.

I was afraid the Worthingtons would use us in some way that Lucien didn't seem to fear. Lucien had the right to do anything he liked, but I did not believe he liked what he had been led to do. For him to get home and be what he had set out to be, discover what that was, would do for him what had never been done for me. And give him a chance I hadn't had.

I would have liked to live my marriage through instead of cutting it off.

He wouldn't understand that. No sex and no conversation with Lucien now. It wasn't part of the deal we had going.

We took a single room at the Six Dollar Six Motel because there was no point wasting more money. I didn't know how much all this would cost before it was done. The room had two beds and a TV between them. I switched on the television. Lucien watched a World War II movie from J. Arthur Rank (Boing! Boing! went the oiled slave on the gong) and I fell asleep immediately, defensive sleeping. The usual dreams of loss.

When I waked at dawn, Lucien was staring at me from his bed. He was naked, the sheet thrown off, his head on his hand, his head and hand on the pillow, and he seemed very serious about trying to figure out what I was doing. I was sleeping. I was waking. His eyes were like a child's, unsmiling. He asked no questions, but he wanted to know more. I didn't know more, either. It was chilly in there. He hadn't understood about the thermostat and he must have been cold. He had been engaged, perhaps, in defensive wakefulness. The light outside, gray of dawn and purple of neon, seeped through the window, under the blinds, and I knew I would be unhappy, gloomed out, shouldn't say a word—had been dreaming again about my marriage—until the sun began to rise and the horizon over the desert turned pink and I found some coffee, dollar flapjacks, eggs, more coffee. "Let's get up. Let's get going," I said.

"I have been ready," he said. "I find I do not need to sleep in North America."

"Do you need to eat?"

"In North America there is food in little packages everywhere."

I liked him. He surprised me, a good reason to help him. If I had been bored, I could just do good for the sake of doing good. It was better to like him. I would prefer this without too much mingling of our bodies and souls.

Friendship might be possible if we didn't grow heavy, distracted, and anxious.

I didn't want to bc a Christian on this carth. Pcrhaps in my afterlife, I might convert and go to heaven.

Or the Ford might give me enough trouble to carry me down into the real world, not the outerspace one of the Interstate, until we had to deal with the Worthingtons once more. While waiting, I would dine on the little packages of roadside food, microwave food in Port-A-Pack trays, get healthy, stay strong, not worry, be prepared, get ready. We were pulling on our clothes. Lucien: Please help by being a little more fun.

"Do you ever have fun?" he asked.

"Just what I was thinking," I said.

"Do you enjoy . . . enjoyment?"

"Enjoyment?"

"La chose," he said winsomely.

"With women," I said.

"So do I," he said. "And with others, too, when necessary."

"I enjoy sleeping." I hoped to slow down his line of argument. "I dream about the past and future. Why didn't you sleep?"

"I dream about the present," he said. "I need little rest. I am mobilized."

Mobilized to let me do all the work while he smiles and watches me. Some mobilization.

"You are sarcastic," he said. He read my thoughts. "Why bother to help me? You say again, helping yourself?"

I shrugged. I buttoned.

"Sad with yourself?"

I shrugged.

"And your dreams of other times and places? You need to pay better attention."

"Let's go." I didn't need lectures from him. "I'm watching out for those who might choose to kill me and hurt you, my friend. How much other attention should I pay? Let's get moving."

"Of course. You are afraid? I hope you have enough courage to be afraid."

"Stipulate, Lucien, that I'm scared shitless. *Move.*"

I bowed him out the door and he caught the joke, double-bowing back at me like a dancer, and we carried our few belongings to the Ford, which seemed already sunk in motel parking lot dust, cans of Tab sprouting near the rear bumper during the night, an empty stretchpants package stuck like a parking ticket under the windshield wiper. I removed it with two fingers and invisible teenagers screamed from the prefab bunker next door. Not only did they go to a motel to fuck; they also went there to play their other teenage games.

We were in the automobile and heading out of the no-town turnoff in which we had spent a night on the road, and straight ahead down a straight road through the desert, and the ear muck of top-forty radio washed over us, turned up by the driver because he was tired of trying to get something more from Lucien. Lucien understood the loud music and talk. He wanted to be silent, too. That fear and hope and intelligence which I had seen briefly boiling in him was settled into drear. I suppose he was also mightily scared, like me. And like me, he didn't like admitting it.

Toward Albuquerque the Ford was squeaking and sagging around turns. I didn't know what broken shock absorbers could do except make us uncomfortable, but when a blue and white sign said, *All American and Foreign Shocks Replaced*, I decided to replace the shocks. I imagined the Ford bumping with one final jar against the ground, the hull scraping against a shallow bottom. It would take a few hours. They would never look for us in Albuquerque, would they? Perhaps delaying to the port would just tucker them out more than we were tired out.

Drunken Indians.

"Do you want Steady Rider Shocks?" the shocks specialist asked me.

"That's me."

" 'Cause I got cheaper, sir. I also got heavy-duty for special weight in the front you carrying."

"Steady Rider sounds okay to me."

He looked at me, at the car, at Lucien. He wore a blue Penney's workshirt with an All-American tag on it. "That's a careful choice," he said, "for a cautious investor in high-grade shock absorbers."

I absorbed the compliment gracefully, I think.

Drunken Indians in front of the swinging door of the Rialto Bar at the corner.

"Be about an hour?" I asked.

"Uh." He looked long and hard down the street to the McDonald's. "You can get a McMuffinburger, whatever they call it, and then you can get a few beers. You got time. You can take in a . . . I guess the movies is closed just now. You and him traveling together? I guess you just might could find something to do. Sir."

Lucien did not look like a homosexual, a genuine black man, or an albino, but this shocks specialist saw difference. He was about to tell us where we could have our beers in the afternoon. He was going to keep talking till he figured us out or we told him.

"I think we'll have a look at the sights of Albuquerque," I said. "Come on, Lucien."

"There are some other beauties here," the shocks man called after us.

Drunk Indians. I had forgotten how the grease in the body floats, stiffening, to the legs and butt when you sit long hours cross-country at the wheel of a car. I was a boy who wanted to rove, arms sailing, alone, in the country, where a boy doing such would dream about finding a pretty girl under a tree, and I said to Lucien, "Let's have a walk. Show you Albuquerque."

"Is this Alba Querk an Indian word?"

"Or Spanish. Both live here, Indians and Mexicans, Anglos. Let's just see if there's something besides McDonald's and Auto Repair."

"There is a bistro," he said, "no doubt there is."

Of course I had traveled country like this before, hunting for dark and cool places to eat. My wife and I had driven across deserts to California and away, found spaghetti joints in small towns, filled ourselves with pasta and wine, and fallen heavily against each other in the motels of this going-someplace land. And slept. And awakened. Once it was still dark, we crept out in towels, we swam naked in the pool with its circlets of suntan oil, and then we ran barefoot back, shivering within our towels, and crawled over each other as if love were the only mountain worthy of climbing in this country.

"You don't know what this is like for me," I said to Lucien.

"You don't know what I am like."

"I'd like you to be a little, oh, polite."

He shrugged. "I think you are saving me from a fate worse than death," he said. "Again and again I died, and now you save me. Am I not courteous?"

And so we got in the Ford and drove. The hood flew up in Oklahoma. I found a welding shop to weld the catch, and wondered if it would hold, because the welder emitted sparks from his machine, the welding flame sizzled, and he didn't take his eyes from the white man traveling with the silent young black man. I hoped he was a professional about welding.

If the hood flew up in my face when the catch broke again, I might smash into an abutment or a tree and die with this man in the car with me. If I died for one of my many mistakes, I could also rid myself of my ghost. What odd appetites. Once I desired pleasure with her, to climb with pleasure over her, to burst with pleasure within her. And now I want silence from her memory. Once I wanted, when I knew I could no longer possess her, to trick and laugh and lose memory with the creatures who had made a captive of Lucien. And now I just wanted to portage the river of America and detrack those creamy, nervous, calculating, crooked colleagues of mine.

Now I was crazed by loneliness. Lucien was less and less help. I didn't like him very much at the moment. But I was still alive and moving, thanks to him.

I worried about the welded catch on the hood as we crossed the Mississippi south of Memphis.

May I die in love again with that lady?

No. I am only permitted to die by myself.

I'm not quite ready yet.

That night in a motel in sight of a rainbow arch across the plain. I awoke suddenly from a dream of nothing, of my wife and nothing, of a tray I was carrying, filled with ashes, and her lovely face open and smiling at me and backing away from me . . . and the bed across the lamp and table in the motel room was empty. The covers were mussed. I was awake. Lucien was gone.

I got up and looked in the bathroom. Empty.

I went to the door marked *Please Leave Your Key* and opened it to look outside, no Lucien, and then closed it quickly. I was naked at a parking lot at one a.m. I dressed. My feet across loose rocks. I headed for the bar, Tony's, and on a Tuesday night the purple neon martini glasses could give a person glaucoma if he stared at them. There was space for a trio on weekends. No trio tonight. *Wilbur & Friends Two on Weekends.* The long curving bar of genuine formica was nearly empty. The bartender was

151

wiping. At the end of the bar, around the curve, as if hiding, sat Lucien with a young man in a tan leisure suit. They were talking. The young man used his little finger to stir his drink.

I thought, We could be seen!

I thought, What's the harm? They wouldn't be following us on these roads.

I went back to bed. I dreamt of trays of ashes. In my dream I groaned, and groaning woke me up, and the bed nearby was still empty, and I willed myself to sleep again and to dream of the cool, loving eyes of someone when she loved me. I could not bring that gaze back. I dreamt again of ashes.

What kind of man can no longer even dream of love?

When I awoke in the morning it was because the door had opened and shut, a narrow gray light striking me across the eyes. I heard footsteps leaving. I looked to the other bed. Lucien was watching me with his eyes aslit from bed-clothes tumbled like the hills of Haiti seen from the air. He grinned. "You never even woke up," he said.

I said nothing.

"I watched," he said, "to see he did not take your purse."

"My wallet."

"He is an honest young man, but I made sure to watch."

I stood up and said, "Come on. This night's over."

**21** A truck stop on the Interstate? No such thing. A Howard Johnson's, with separate asphalt field for the browsing semis and diesel lower-space lumbering heavies. They kept their motors running, some of them, to keep the air conditioning going in their foam bunks behind the steering compartment. A girl with a short black skirt was wandering among the trucks, high heels, hair bubbled over, vinyl portfolio of purse—something you'd get out of a vending machine in the ladies' room—and there were others like her (tights, hot pants, belly buttons winking) and Lucien asked me, "Where are we?"

"In a state someplace in the middle. I'm tired."

"You wish to sleep again?" he asked mildly.

"When I'm tired, I drink coffee."

"For me this is very interesting," he said, "more interesting than coffee. You will drink coffee and I will examine these trucks." There were smells of oil and rubber and stagnant water.

"Examine good," I said, "but you're not in business."

The day-glo orange interiors of the eating facility had been replaced by Early American Coffeehouse Knotty

Pine. There were shingles above eye level. Plastic and vinyl kept personal contact neat, clean, and shiny, with muted colonial-era colors. The cash register emitted computer beeps. I finished my cup and the one free refill. Lucien and I were like two teenagers wandering down a beach together, our ears glued to different transistors. I had no idea what was in his mind. He had a distorted idea of what was in mine. Even I had unclear ideas of my own thoughts. But somehow, because I thought Lucien more whole than I was, or maybe just younger, or at least he deserved the chances I had failed for forty years, I was putting myself out for him. It made no difference who deserved what or why. I wanted to do it. For my own sake, as a last chance, that's enough. And I had left him among those heavy trucks for no good reason but sleepiness and not paying attention. I left my cup sloshing in its saucer. I stood up in a hurry, bellying the counter.

Out in the pasture of the great trucks, smelling of oil and exhaust and that steamy, gritty dampness where a radiator had overflowed with a gusher of rust, I found Lucien backed against a huge wheel by a man in cigar, Can't-Bust-'Ems, and a gun in his belt. He had not pulled the weapon yet. As I yelled, "Wait a sec!" he was saying, "No ID?"

"What is that?"

"No identification papers, buster?"

"He's with me," I said.

The man turned, smiling and drawling, "Is you an identification paper, uncle?"

"Now wait a sec—sir—I have his papers right here."

The man showed his teeth. "You got his papers. That's wonderful. I'm a reasonable man though a deputy, I don't want no trouble, uncle. You got his papers, so I'll only haul his ass in for trespassing and disturbing the peace."

"What the fuck's on your mind?" I inquired.

"Watch it! Watch it!" And he pulled his pistol.

154

"I'm sorry, Mister Deputy," I said, "I was just worried is all, and you're not dressed like an officer—"

"Plain clothes. We get a rotten element around here."

"I see that now. And I been driving without enough sleep, not even shaving very much, I do realize, and it's kind of worrisome to find my young friend here backed up like this—what'd he do?"

"Soliciting, maybe. I don't know what the fuck kind of miscreant he is, he's weird."

"Would you like me to get you the papers?"

"Aw, I suppose."

But I was sure the tourist papers I had would be Esperanto to this fellow. I preferred to try talking him over. Or perhaps buying him over. "Here's my driver's license," I said. I handed him my wallet with a twenty-dollar bill tucked behind the license. He examined the document. He examined the bill. He seemed to read off the numbers. He studied President Jackson. He sighed and handed them all back to me separately, wallet, driver's license, and twenty-dollar bill.

"Tell you what," he said. "I don't want no necessary trouble. The on-necessary trouble is bad enough. So you take your things, and just give me my little thing—"

If he doesn't want money? I thought.

"I'm a fairy copmother," he said, and he leaned forward, spitting first on the ground, and pressed his lips against Lucien's, heaving his beef hard against Lucien, grunting with the sudden heavy movement of a man used to forgetting his wishes in food, beer, and malevolence.

I was about to pull him off by his fur, but I didn't have the chance. He suddenly crumpled to the ground, jerking head and knees together, curled like a Can't-Bust-'Em fetus, and Lucien touched his knee as if to check on the damage from stroking a man's genitals with a knee cap. Ah, ah, ah, the man was gasping. In a moment he would get his voice. "Come on!" I said, but then stopped, plucked out his pistol, and heaved it under the truck. "Come on!"

We ran for our car and (thank you, Ace) the motor turned over.

Down the highway, five miles over fifty-five, I thought: He won't make a big deal of it. He won't follow. And I said: "Why'd you do that?"

"Why did he do that?" Lucien asked.

"New habits that I know of out here," I said. "Did you give him some sort of signal?"

"For that?"

"No, I suppose not," I said.

Maybe the guard just knew. Maybe he didn't know. I drove.

I was with Priscilla, and we hurtled silently, slowly, through space; we were enclosed together in our carapace, part of a single organism on the highway; and we talked and laughed, or we fell silent and listened to the all-states radio, the squawk from Texas or Chicago of music and selling; many times we couldn't wait till night, we stopped, we made love in the grass by the roadside, we clutched and felt each other wetly like teenagers in the car, we stopped and I said, What the hell, and we registered in a motel for an hour or two, a shower, a sleepy continuing of our voyage across America.

Not so with Lucien. The space between us grew larger. Like a father, I felt dislike for a sulky child; like a child, he felt bored and resentful. We hurtled through space as strangers. I tried to remember why I was doing this; and when I could no longer remember, I thought only: One time I have to finish what I start. I need to be on track again.

Not enough, but I felt justified and lean. This alertness was not necessarily nervous. The tiny satisfaction of crossing county lines with Spanish and Indian names was intact. *Leaving Putah County. Welcome to El Adobe County. You are now leaving El Adobe County. Welcome to ...* The larger satisfaction of crossing state boundaries (okay, I've covered that one, and now for the next one). I would never come back this way again.

Lucien was standing at the grand console in a men's room, plugging in coins for combs, key chains, Kleenex, disposable toothbrush, miniature playing cards, hand lotion in palm-sized squeeze bottle, map, chocolate-covered raisinettes, gum, two squirts of cologne—practically everything a man doesn't really need.

He said, "I found this!"

"Where the hell were you?"

"Look what I found. I was here."

"I didn't see you."

He smiled. Of course. Why didn't I see him? I imagined flight or disaster, but he was only catching a cloud of cologne in the face.

In the southwest, where Lucien might have taken to looking like an Indian, turquoise bracelets and an inscrutable face, or dusty jeans and a scrutable face, instead he seemed to be trying out for traveling salesman: beads of sweat on the forehead and shirt pocket sagging with pens. "Twelve for a dollar, all different colors," he said.

Maybe it made him feel safer, less black, less tracked. But no one but me is blinded by a pocketful of pens.

"Get back in the car. Lucien, don't you want to get home?"

"Yes. I am going there."

"Maybe," I said. "It's up to me, isn't it?"

He didn't look insulted. He assented to this. It was up to me. He climbed in and rubbed his knee where he had bumped it.

157

He no longer looked at me full in the face. There was something girlish about how he didn't look at me. Of course, we were sitting side by side and he would have to turn to look at me, and I had to keep my eyes on the road, so why was I bothered so? Would it have been girlish and flirtatious if he had kept trying to catch my eye? But now he avoided looking at me.

I drove. As I switched from a rock station to a news station, I heard the words "—of natural causes," and I would never know who had died or what natural causes are. I think it's never natural.

Our bodies are filled with natural causes.

The world is filled with natural causes just waiting to explode.

**22** "You are awake to drive?" Lucien asked.
"Awake enough."
"Good. Then I sleep," he said, and turned half on his side, his hands warmed between his knees, his head bobbing slightly with the motion of travel.

The roadway hummed by our stationary vehicle. Speed got us noplace. I drove.

Boredom used to make me indignant. The world owed me fun and sex, money and delight—distractions everywhere, plus true love around the corner. Now I wasn't even indignant at the notion that enemies might hurt me, kill me, a distraction I didn't need. Indignation suffered a power failure at the thought Lucien might be stolen at the final moment in Miami. Amid palm trees, someone could run me down with a car; slug me, knife me, shoot me; in the international glass-and-aluminum airport, a Cuban might stick me with acid, poison, or explosives—no indignation.

I had just set myself a task. And not even for money.

Is this age? Is this what I do when I'm only doing my time? But no one but me had told me what my job was; they had told me it was other.

Copiously the carburetor pumped gas through the engine. Wasting and flooding and spending were what I was doing. I was soothed. I was bored with danger and the carelessness of our fleeing. Lucien's little smile and his silence confirmed what we both knew. He had a right to a grudge against me for making his decisions.

Deserts. Desert towns with assembly plants. Rexco. *Serving the Southwest since 1963.* The Mississippi. Humid river towns, serving the valley since forever. High cattails of grain, corn and wheat. The freeways, the Interstate, the freeway. In offramp settlements there was food in little packets, unwrapped, moving stately through the body to be excreted the next day in another Howard Johnson's, Wendy's, Jack in the Box, or Sambo's, further disentangled from invisible casings by the body's secretions and labors. Lucien seemed to doze across America. I thought he was the sort to be interested, but he was interested in something else, his dreams—of Kenscoff? of what did a village boy dream?—while I was trying to stop dreaming of the woman I had lost. He slept, he woke, he peed and shat, he sniffed the air like an animal, he ate. I drove.

He looked into my face a moment with a little smile. All this was my business, not his. I drove.

He stretched his arms and legs and yawned. Pink tongue like anyone else's. He roamed around the car at gas stations like an animal exploring his territory. Then he slept and I drove.

Once when I changed my order from scrambled eggs to poached, I saw a waitress tip her chin up and make a little disgusted tccchping sound with her tongue and teeth. It was the sound my wife used to make when I failed to live up to her expectations in some matter (remember the laundry, remember to shop, remember to make her come). I wondered what sound this waitress would make when she was really happy and delighted by a man, and he didn't need to work for this result. "He wanna change his order, too?" she asked, tccchping at Lucien.

160

My job was to drive. Maybe we would escape the Worthingtons.

When I felt pain, I wanted to cry but no longer knew how. I was cured and freeze-dried in time. My eyes ached, my temples ached, my brain strained to grow a tumor and pressed against the bone. The frontal lobe swelled. I had longed to hold her in my arms; what a simple hunger and impossible of answer.

So I was busy with these deeds.

Loneliness had made me stiff and solemn in my cottage on Princess Street in Bernal Heights in San Francisco. I wanted to break my luck. I had once been a boy long past my time, but then I had fallen in love and lost her, and then I was gray, pompous, sarcastic, with long creases in my cheeks, parentheses around my mouth; and even when I talked or laughed, I didn't rest my eyes on another's eyes. I looked away. I couldn't see what wonders other eyes still possessed; I saw spiders on the wall. I was missing something. I remembered her well-bred bray when she was happy, amused, that once amused, healthy, departed wife.

So I went on stubbornly doing foolish things, living day by day. And hearing that well-bred bray as an echo in the night, when it awakened me in dreams I could not remember.

So I did what I did. Driving.

Like others, I had imagined love and got marriage. I had imagined a girl, a woman, and found my particular creature wife. What she dreamed of and rejected she never described. She was too polite for that, although she yelled in a fury of goading about my teeth, my moles, my person that she once loved to kiss and lick. She said she was sorry for yelling, a little upset about wanting never to see me again. It was just a way of saying good-bye. She didn't really care about my missing toe. I was just irritating, that's all.

So I carried Lucien, not sure he needed this.

Flashing glints of sunrise beneath the trees along the highway, in the rolling worn hills of the south heading east, was the best news of a day which used to be filled with good news—leaves, tastes, sounds, my walking on the planet as a self-employed veteran, pompous with love. I had loved her.

It was no longer the story of my life. This is the story of my life. My life of light and love is over. This is the story of my life. Yet I was still glad when we stopped to piss on the rear tire, eat at Sambo's.

I was doing something she never chose for me. Good.

I wish I could choose more freely for myself.

Lucien was like a wife, wasn't he? Was that why he laughed at me for rescuing him from another man? In the silence of the Interstate, he thought we were free of the Worthingtons. I kept my foot on the accelerator at acceptable speed, five miles above the posted limit. The cramp in my foot extended to the toe which was no longer there. I drove.

I had a plan: Park the Ford at the Miami Airport and never see it again. It could sit there, filled with old Kleenex and sandwich wrappings, its guts frayed by feet, underpins eaten by winter salt and southwest sand, until they towed it away. Lucien would be home and I would be wherever I found myself next. By that time I would surely have a new plan.

We were driving among palm trees. Why are they ominous? I never expect anything good to happen among palm trees. We had made it safely across America, and now the palm trees were come to get us. They looked dusty and knobby and spiky, in this pearly-gray clime, tropical industrial southland filled with smog, Florida at last . . .

"We also talk to ourselves at night in Haiti," Lucien said. "There is no light. Maybe there is nobody to talk to except the loa. We pray the ghosts and the zombis do not talk back."

"I'm sorry."

"Perhaps you would like to talk with me?"

"Would you listen?"

"I do not know, if I must be honest. I try."

"I'll take that offer under consideration," I said. He looked to see if my lips were moving, and since they weren't, he shut his eyes, pretending to doze or dozing. I drove. I didn't beat my chest. I didn't have the vapors. I drove an old Ford with a foreigner who slept a lot. Perhaps he knew I couldn't explain to him what more we were doing than avoiding the deals we had made.

There used to be women around here. Around here was around me, when I was doing the wrong things. Now I was doing the right thing and there was no woman around me. If I slept—ah, there's a copcar warily hiding in traffic, wondering if I'll wobble like that again—maybe I could get out of the trouble I was bringing down.

"The officer would not search us, would he?" Lucien asked.

"Christ, what are you carrying?"

"You know."

"You carrying something?"

"Nothing. A little hashish."

I lifted my sore foot to bring the speed down. If they gave tickets for Chinese caution at the wheel, I would do thirty days in the county farm. "You dump that stuff next gas station where we stop right away."

"Maybe we get high together."

"You dump it or I'll dump you!"

"Could you do that?" he mildly inquired.

"Oh Christ!" I asked the steering wheel, pounding it. "You've had this for three thousand miles of Arizona, Texas—shit! I may have to slug you and take it from you."

"I don't think that should be done," Lucien said.

The cop seemed to give up, he turned into the outside lane in a wide dramatic fast arc and roared past, eying me with disgust for not helping in his deep-felt need to cite me; he sped ahead, tracking other prey. I felt weak in the belly. I pulled onto the offramp and wheeled into the gas station, self-service zone. I switched off the motor and put the key in my pocket. "Give it to me."

"What?"

"The stuff."

"Give you what?"

No explanations. I grabbed his head and let it go. The burry stiff curly hair. "Get out," I said.

He looked at me as if I were crazy; he climbed out of the Ford, yawning and stretching. "Give it to me!" I said.

"Ah. No."

I jumped out, grabbed him again, and started to go through his pockets. He let me. I knew he could hurt me if he wanted to, I could hurt him if I wanted to, but he let me just dig for the little brown plastic vial. He had it in concentrated oil form.

"You don't want that," he said.

"*You* don't want it. Was it a little something from your Palm Springs owner? He put it in your pants for you? I'll tell you what. We'll plant it in the garden there behind the station."

"Pardon?"

But I was already walking back and digging at the loose sod with my feet and I buried the plastic bottle. "Compromise," I said. "So it'll grow. So if you come this way again you can dig it up or harvest the hashish tree in this spot."

He made a sickly smile, one corner up, one corner down. He knew a joke when it came his way, but he didn't necessarily like it. He shrugged. Okay, Dr. Bonni had been good to him, even if he used a razor blade on his skin now and then. Maybe he would come this way without me some time. Dr. Bonni made these little oozing skin cuts, but he cared. Did I care?

Lord, are you listening? I thought. What is the meaning of life? But please make it brief, because I'm in a hurry.

Someplace within I was full of pep for the trouble I had earned. Come on, I'm ready to rock. I had spent the beginning of this job still missing the lady I loved, and then enjoying the tastes of the women I didn't love, who circulated around this peculiar money, and now the money and the women were gone and I was a driver. I was transport. My cargo was inert; I'm not sure I was ert. It was too late even to regret my life; I could imagine no other. The heat of asphalt, of the roads of this country, was bubbling up over the land, the Ford, the palm trees, Lucien, and me. I felt enveloped in lassitude, and full of pep, as if these contrary nerves had been like the driving, a kind of sleep. When I was supposed to be in fear, I was now waiting for the Worthingtons, who would be waiting for me someplace.

But philosophy takes second place, doesn't it, to the cop from the highway ambling around the self-service stand of the HoJo barracks, leaning on his hip in that way they have, prosthetic copness holding them up, asking, "What you fellows doing back here? Don't you answer, white guy." His stare pointed toward the damp mound of churned-up earth. "Funny-looking black kid, *you* answer."

Lucien grinned. "Peepee," he said.

The cop wrinkled his nose at the dampness. "The johnnies inside not good enough for you boys?"

I waited. He looked at us with joyful superiority, face-meat glowing.

"Okay," he said, "I guess this is no worse'n a rear tire. Get on now."

We started walking.

His voice followed us. "Okay, I do you a favor, you think? You think wrong. You tell yourself lies. You in lots of trouble. You tell lies," and laughter followed us.

"You think that was a true police?" Lucien asked.

When I looked at Lucien, I no longer saw Lucien's face. I

165

looked into something so familiar I knew it no longer. And this face wanted to tell me something, but I couldn't hear it. Yet I would play out the game I had started, stubborn I was. I didn't even know what I could win or lose. If it was my life, I was ready.

The cop's eyes were watching us in the dark.

Just before my wife left, she had surprised me. She had been hurting me with silence and withdrawal. I had begun to see someone prepared only for perfection and I wouldn't do. And then one morning in our earthquake cottage she had awakened me with her soft tongue working at my crotch, it felt like the holy center of my being as I came out of what dream, I didn't remember what dream, her licking and kissing and taking. And then she thrashed when I thrashed, and she came smiling up to my mouth, kissing me so that I tasted my own seed in her mouth, and then I fell asleep again. She had always said she wasn't ready to have children. She moved out after the briefest of explanations the next evening. *I'm not ready to settle for you, Sid* . . .

Lucien was still watching the cop circling in his car on the slick black of the parking lot.

The cop was watching us still.

"Let's go," I said.

"If you please," said Lucien.

From here I thought to drive due south nonstop to Miami, through a thickening traffic of out-of-state sun-seekers. "You are hurrying so," Lucien said.

"This ain't for fun."

He curled up, his hands in askew prayer formation under his ear.

"You're not going to sleep again," I said.

He didn't answer.

"You can't be sleeping," I said. "It's another joke you're playing."

166

We had to stop one last time. The body endures, but the gas tank has no will; it will not consume itself. *TROUT OIL AND MINI SUPERETTE, Food Gas Tums, Friendliness Is Our Sign.* I pulled up to the pump.

"Fill her up, please."

The attendant stared at Lucien and shook her head.

"Is this self-serve?"

"No, I was just wondering. Is that shirt Native American? That a Seminole shirt I never seen?"

"Fill her up, please."

She started to unhook the nozzle. This was full service. Car, smell that nice fresh gas. She came around and motioned to me. I leaned toward her. "Uh, sir?" she asked. She watched Lucien get out, sleepily untangling himself, lips pouting with fatigue; he straightened up and stretched, first right, then left; he headed for the men's. "Sir?" she asked.

"What?"

"Are you a Pisces? Because I can hack it with Pisceans."

"Could you check my oil?"

"You're really into checking your oil, aren't you? I'm a Capricorn. Only certain men please me. You're half a quart low. How come you two, that black boy, I see he is, now I see it, you traveling together like that? You friends?"

"Yes, yes, thank you."

She made the Ballantine Beer sign. "I can dig it," she said, "partner. We here in the New American southland are not so dumb and backwards as your license plate would lead me to believe you believe."

"I believe," I said, paying cash. "I dig." I had never met an astrologer without eyelashes before.

I got out and moved toward the Mini Superette.

"You want to look for your black boy?" she asked.

He hadn't gone to the men's room yet. He was standing in these vague hills, with this shiny black snake of highway circling around us, interchange, offramp somethingette, studying the sights. In his silence and watching, travel-stained, his smile like a snarl or a bite, he was like a stray dog I was trying to tame. Not nice of him to make me feel that way. Not nice of a dog to stray. But dogs do that.

When he left for the washroom, I wondered if he would return and he didn't. So I pulled the Ford away from the pump and went to reattach the leash. There was a swirling turnaround of tiremarks in the lot. Heat rising from asphalt with a greasy, salty, chemical smell. Lucien was standing there as if in the center of a target, looking at the vague soft American freeway slopes. "Where are you going?" I asked. "You ain't goin' nowhere."

He turned and stared. How rare that he ever looked into my eyes. Now he resolved to look and stared.

"I wish to speak seriously at last," Lucien said. "We are nearly there, where you are leading me."

"I wish to listen seriously," I said. I motioned him to sit on the cement ridge at the edge of the lot. He did not. I did, then stood up again.

"You have been playing a game."

"I've been trying to help you."

"So I thought in California several days ago. Now I think you do not mind if you are killed, and with you, me." I had nothing to say. "But I mind," he said. "For me, my life is not a game."

"You treated it that way."

"If you think it was sport, no. I was poor and ignorant. Such persons do not make the same entertainments with their lives which—"

"Which people like me do."

"Yes. Which people like you play with people like me."

"Do you think the Worthingtons or your fancy razor-blade collector in Palm Springs weren't playing games? And why were you carrying that little bottle of oil?"

168

"I understand the rules a little. I know a little of what they want. I also make mistakes. I thought they were my enemy and you my friend."

"And now you don't know?"

"Does a friend lead me toward my enemies without telling me what he wants from my risk? Ah, you take risk, too. But for some reason it pleases you. I come along like your slave, Meester Kasdan, I just come along with you because you please to trade me for something else you want."

"Rather odd of you to think of it that way, Lucien."

"I do not escape slavery no matter what I do. My rescuer is also a trader. But he does not tell me the price or what he gains."

He could not be expected to be grateful. I could not expect him to be my friend. One of the things I must have wanted was gratitude; otherwise, why this deadness in my heart? If I could let him do something for me, help me, rescue me, as in fact he was doing, he could allow us to be friends. But how was he ever to know how I needed him? I was simply carting him someplace while he gave me his knowledge: I carried him for my own reasons. This was the truth which occupied a sleepy person who had let me harass him across America.

"What can you do for me?" I asked him.

I knew what I had already done for Lucien. I was responsible for breaking his deal. The Worthingtons would reach for him, and his only chance was to get back to Kenscoff, where his village might protect him. He wasn't equipped to survive without me until he was home, and it was I who made him naked and defenseless. So why didn't I just leave him be? They might kill him. They would do the same to me. For them, it would have a pedagogical intention, but we would be just as maimed or dead as if they cared about us. But why, at this time in my middle age, should I feel so responsible for either of us?

Well, I liked finishing something by my own choice. Other matters had been finished for me and this had tuckered me out for years. Winning Lucien from the Worthingtons, taking my best shot at it, wasn't such a bad way to end things. He was serving Sid's purposes, too.

"What can I do for you?" he asked.

"You don't have to answer that question."

"You don't even love boys," he said. "For the lovers of boys I can at least do that. For the lovers of money, I can at least be sold. For you, there is only yourself."

There was no way to explain. He was not to touch me. He wanted to despise me because I desired neither money nor his body.

Perhaps he was right. Those at least were desires that can be shared. And now that he was leaking talk, he would not stop. "What right have you to tell me where to go, what to do, even when I want to go to the bathroom? What right have you to rescue me from—" he shrugged "—from nothing. From Docteur Bonni." He leaned toward me and showed his large squarish teeth with the purple gums. "What right have you to make me your own grateful slave?"

I felt dizzy. I was not here. I remembered a woman in Frankfurt. I remembered the men in white linen suits. I remembered remembering my wife. Hadn't he begged for help? Hadn't he let me see him bleeding from razor cuts on his nipples? "Don't," I said.

"If you please," he said, "then I won't." There were purple shadows in the dark skin, dark as a bad orange, beneath his eyes. Not enough exercise; the wrong kind of sleep. The slightly swollen boy's face grew very serious. This face, in the parking lot of the Mini Superette, Food Gas Tums, wished to complete some transaction. Two men were here discussing business with the sun shimmering in a turmoil of heat off the black, soft, hell-smelling asphalt.

170

"What more is on your mind?" I asked.

"Pardon?"

"What else are you trying to say?"

"Très bien." He met my eyes straight, and at last a boyish smile replaced that long-time sullenness. He glinted and made merry at me. His lips pursed and squealed in a little sucking noise. He said, "I do for you now?"

His hand crept toward my pants.

When it touched me, I hit it as hard as I could.

"Ow, ouch, that hurt. Sir, are you being delicate?"

I stared at him. I would not warn him. I would not hit him. I would not abandon him. I could not explain to him.

"Get in the car, we're going," I said.

"Are you sure, my dear guardian?"

"Enough of this foolishness."

"Are you sure that was enough? Only that was enough for you?"

"Get in."

He shrugged. He didn't know what I wanted any better than I did. But that was not what I wanted.

Now we would not stop until we reached the Miami Airport.

**23** I parked in the short-term lot, near the blackish puffs of jet fuel, with a nice extravagant sense of saving money because I would never pay this parking fee. I was driving a throwaway car. It was disposable, like Kleenex, in my present extravagant need. I left it, and someday they would tow it away to sell at a police sale, and I doubted if anyone would try to find the previous owner. Computers have better things to do with their time. When they found the car, what it could tell the Worthingtons would be small details about ancient history. I kind of liked the idea of the bishop and his brother ignorant about small matters.

Since our talk in the parking lot of the Mini Superette, Food Gas Tums, Lucien had kept the peace. He watched without a word while I bought tickets on Delta to Port-au-Prince. Modestly he stared into middle space while I counted out the bills. He was interested in the parade of travelers. When a stewardess glanced at us, a white man traveling with a black man, a harassed middle-aged man with a pretty young one, I stared back. She opened her teeth. "I suppose you're from New Orleans," she said sweetly, "or San Francisco."

172

I must have looked worried about whether I would get what I wanted. Lucien's little smile and silence looked as if he knew what he was getting. Perhaps he did. Silence and peace come to the man who has no further choice to make. Say this for me: I was worried and uncalm and still trying. The stewardess with the blazing teeth might want to say less than this for me, but she turned to say more to her friend, a blue-clad Pan Am stew with little wheels on her suitcase.

"On nous remarque," said Lucien.

"We must be remarkable, my friend."

A nonsmell of chrome, glass, steel, aluminum, and air conditioning filled my nose, but beyond the layers of product I felt a tropical weight of flowers, rot, papaya, and a fertile crop of people rising all about us, narrow-hipped Cubans in high heels, thighs and boots working, short fat legs and speedy long legs, kid vacationers with guitars, off-duty stews with blue Pan Am bags and bodies fresh out of uniform, tourists, business travelers with business packaging, briefcases, NoDoz, Valium, and underarm protection, folks who had a good reason, better reasons than mine, for all this scuffling.

Behind the photography stand—*Drop Off Your Film, Receive It By Mail*—in a hustle of transport, I felt footsteps on target. Echo slapped sandals toward us. A smiling shaven head approached with its body hidden by a burden of saffron robes, rotogravure magazines, a flower, a declaration ripe on its parted lips. Hare Krishna, brother. But this was not a Hare Krishna. The fetal head approached; the legs were trotting; soft high-laced black boots appeared between the folds of the robe; something smelled of patchouli oil. "Won't you," he asked, "please accept this token of love from the Celestial Education Foundation?"—pushing, pushing, toward Lucien a flower on a long blue-headed pin.

"Run!" I said.

Lucien hurtled alongside me toward the gate, his heels clattering. It was easy. The monk, hobbled by his robes, scampered a few steps and then gave up. "Hare Krishna anyway, brother," he called, "tu es foutu."

"I believe he is Haitian," Lucien said.

I said, "You're sure of that, so why do you say believe?"

We stood at the security line and I congratulated myself for not being winded. Well, I hadn't sprinted very much and there had been no determined effort to catch us. The monk was not a running poisoner. But my heart was loud in my chest from the exertion of fear. There were too many people here. All of them belonged to the Worthingtons. The one behind me tapped my shoulder and I whirled. She had tears in her eyes. Luci hugged me clumsily with all our hard luggage in the way; she kissed me; her cheeks were wet.

"Why you?" I said.

"I'm so glad. I'm so glad," she said.

"Do you think you can help me?" I asked.

"Maybe I can hinder you," she said. "Please. Don't think I'm not still your friend, I am, Sid. Please don't hurt yourself."

She clung to my arm. I was much less afraid of myself than of her. Yet tears are always sincere, aren't they? Lucien didn't seem surprised. I would have to accept the fact that Luci had met me. What good would it do to ask how she found me? I wouldn't believe her anyway. "Your flight toward Port-au-Prince is ready. Please move to the boarding area. Votre vol vers Port-au-Prince . . ." My hand luggage floated away through the X-ray machine. I walked under the arching metal detector and my keys made a shrill protest. "Please remove your belt. Please put your keys in the box."

Luci looked at the paper contained with my heap of scrap metal. She looked at my belt with its Southern Pacific buckle. Her tears were quickly replaced by curiosity: a thing to know about her.

"Now walk through again," said a black guard in a green twill suit. "Both of you separately." Lucien waited dutifully behind me. Good boy. "That's better."

Luci caught up with me as I was slipping my belt back on, pocketing my keys. "You're going also?" I said.

"Of course. The weather is perfect in Haiti this time of the year. I was worried about you, Sid."

"I'll bet."

"There is good reason, Sid."

I said nothing. She knew what I thought: that she was providing some of the good reasons. But also Luci seemed to want to do this thing, to tell me she was glad I lived and she would be sorry if I ceased to do so. I have done some bad things—losing the woman I loved, choosing the wrong ways to love, and I still haven't learned about small matters, also. What to think about Luci. Whether to rush into mortal peril. If I was wrong about the woman I had trusted with my life, why couldn't I be wrong about Luci, whom I trusted to betray me?

I had been teaching Lucien to trust me, which meant preparing him with misinformation about the world. He was taking to asking me questions, as if this is how one prepares to board a plane to Haiti.

"You are North American, of course?"

"Of course."

"You are stubborn and not a reasonable person?"

"I'm on time. I listen to reason when I have to."

"I thought you were supposed to be clever?"

"I used to be, in a way."

"Do you do good for yourself?"

"No. No. Good point. But I used to think I did."

"So in the important way, you are not clever. You are willing to give up your life for me."

"For a reason, Lucien."

"Why? Explain, please."

But he required no answer. He looked bored. A grayness came over his face, the opposite of a flush on that freakish pale Haitian skin, a violet look under light coffee color. "I suppose I do not need to understand the difference among white men."

"Not to do what you're doing."

"As you like," he said politely.

I would not stop to ask just now what he liked and what I liked. We were being followed. Footsteps scattered themselves behind us and pushed through the line where we waited to board. I wondered if there were taps on his heels. Then I felt the breath on my neck. "Sir? Would you help out a poor soul who . . ."

"Who what?" With a line like that, he needed at least to complete his sentence.

"Who needs shelter for the night." He beamed at Lucien. He negotiated with me. "I do triples. Maybe you've never had a triple. It's an enjoyment, sir."

He was wearing a white turtleneck with smudges of soot at the collar and white patches under the arms. It must have looked elegant, furry, and woolen, hanging on a mannequin. It looked less elegant now. Why were we being held? Why was everyone so patient, shifting parcels, letting anybody at all push through to us? I wanted to board. He whispered fiercely, "You didn't even ask how much. Maybe it's free."

I was sure it was.

"What's that?" Lucien asked.

"Good question." I thought I'd try to remember the man for future reference. He was grinning at us with loose pink hippo folds of membrane jiggling in his open mouth. "I don't know you," I said. "That's the truth, Lucien. Maybe he meant whatever he said."

As the line started to move, the man in the white turtleneck pushed alongside us. "Take a meeting," he said. "Please. Right now. Word of honor—" I must have looked doubtful. "Or dishonor, as you prefer, no doubt." He was puffing. He had succeeded in making me listen, a fault I have. "It may be worth your time, sir, and it may even cost you nothing. Anyway, we'll have the flight together, won't we, so we can get to know ourselves?"

We would travel together, all these jokers. They had found us. I couldn't break out of the chain. I decided to follow it to the end and not to leave Lucien, although I doubted I could carry either of us out of the Worthington universe.

Elsewhere, in an elsewhere town, I had asked too much of a wife. Now I asked nothing at all. I pursued small risks, such as the loss of my life, to bring Lucien back home to Kenscoff.

It seemed the exporters were not greedy, either. They had ideals. It wasn't money. It was sport and they just didn't want me to best them.

But they wouldn't play fair despite those scented Episcopal robes. Despite that warmth of her body holding me, my body snug in hers, all that slime of friendly communion, Luci found me disposable. To kill me? Well, why not? Wives kill husbands; husbands kill wives; lovers kill each other with no explanation but that they want to. And Luci had practical reasons. She was ahead of the game.

I said to Lucien, "Watch people here and be like everybody."

"I try to look white," he said. "Look how the curls in my hair are straighter. And is my nose less, less nostrils?"

"You're learning."

"Merci, blanc."

In Creole, blanc doesn't mean just white. It also means stranger. His dewy soft eyes found mine in the press of the line as if he believed eyes are the window of the soul, there

177

is a soul, eyes give the news of the soul; as if all this were true, while finding assigned seating on a 707. It's person-to-person time. His eyes were effective at the practice and perhaps they had gotten him in some of his trouble. Toiling away in the foolishness of feeling, our nails grew, our ears thrummed, our feet were hot in our socks, our bodies felt crowded. We let the Worthingtons welcome us back.

We filed onto the plane which still had the musty smell of its customs disinfecting after the Caribbean run. I saw the Bugfry aerosol can with its cartoon monster flat on his carapace, eleven five-color paws in the air, near the *Reader's Digests* piled above the stewardesses' row of seats. On this flight, our luck, say it slowly please, our luck: returning Haitians with tennis rackets and tennis sweaters, guitars, boxes bound with wire, bottles of scotch, Macy's and Jeans Warehouse plastic bags, the booty of voyaging; very like in their intentions what the tourists bring out of Haiti—goat skins, tin cans battered into the shape of tin lamps, mahogany goblets: *I traveled!* A black diplomat with his bronze wife, a husky, dusky lady out of Curaçao, maybe Dutch and African rather than Afro-Danish, sat a little apart from her and their solemn, cute, overdressed kiddies. He had a briefcase, he leaned toward the aisle, that was what made him seem apart from her, but at takeoff he took her hand and snapped the briefcase shut on its Haitian war secrets. He enveloped her hand to provide temporary immunity to air fright. (*He* was frightened of flying.) There was a crew of American tourists in t-shirts with decal bellies on their real bellies: *Fat Club of Queens*, and the same legend and design, with a black navel, on their white canvas golf hats, bellies on the crowns. A future divorcee, chic in French jeans, Indian gauze shirt, spiked shoes, and a gold wedding band she was about to shed, wept to herself over a copy of *Apartment Life*. After her one-day divorce she would stay a few days, nursing a sore finger from twisting off her ring, and a Haitian cab driver would suck it all better. I read her name stenciled on her denim carryall: Christie. Christie, slip off your heels and get some circulation in your ankles.

"Hi, Christie with an ie," I said.

"How'd you know that?" she sobbed, grieving for lost love and alert to a new one on the longish Caribbean flight. (Not me. But I kind of liked her tiny nose for the short pull.) "So howja know that? I can't converse so good with all this gulping. My ears."

"Eet ees written," said helpful Lucien. He put his hand on my knee to lean over and point to her carryall.

She took note of my pretty Haitian boyfriend, her tears dried by the magic of prurience, and she winked at me.

It was as if that wink lifted a curtain. Too many of my dear friends and colleagues were traveling with me. We were all in the plane and it was filled with the strangers I least would like to know, except perhaps for Luci, and she was sitting in the three abreast coach seats with Lucien and me. Maybe she didn't wish me ill. I might have liked to find out, but just now I was otherwise occupied.

Unless they hijacked the plane (not likely), the Worthingtons probably could do me no ill for awhile. "We are currently flying at an altitude of . . . until we attain our normal cruising speed of . . ." A creative pilot was changing the drone on us. Did the Worthingtons have one of their pilots doing the job? No, he would be programmed for the normal drone. In their normal droning businesslike way, in general, they only wanted to prohibit me. I was not sure I wanted to be prohibited. Perhaps, for them, it was most important to teach their own people about consequences and I didn't really matter. I would play out my time. I was carrying Lucien around like a bottle with my thumb caught in it. I would drag my burden until I or it broke against some obstacle. Why didn't he care? He was study-

179

ing an advertisement for an Exercycle in the flight magazine. A woman in a body stocking was riding it while a man in a warmup suit was waiting his turn in their family room. Lucien had the bland wonderment on his face of a tourist visiting his first voodoo ceremony.

No, it wasn't for the money that I'd gotten into this. It was the boiled murk I was after.

"Murk," I said aloud.

"Pardon?" said Luci.

"I'd like some bouillon," I said. "I can't stand high-altitude coffee."

"Don't you think they do the coffee better on European flights?"

"Just burned and boiled," I said. *"Why did they send you on this trip?"*

"Not only to keep you company, Sid."

"What else?"

"Sales meeting. Re-evaluation of the business. The bishop thinks we should be getting into other things—"

I raised my hand. I didn't want to know. If they told me so easily, it meant they had no intention of ever letting me go.

"Skag," she said. "Coke. Oh, I don't know, maybe used cars. They're all around us, Sid. You're dead if you make trouble."

I sighed and thought it was a good idea to enjoy the world while it was still buzzing and churning about me and my head was intact. She didn't have to tell me. I was probably a future dead man.

These being the facts, I chose to regard a girl with a long and narrow face, high forehead, long very clean American hair tumbling about her shoulders, and I thought: How nice to see her and just think, *How beautiful. How I want her.* And I was thinking maybe I really do want her. And I was busy avoiding the subject, which was that a little group had gotten on the plane without going through the line—of course, first class has a separate ramp—and they were waiting for me. Maybe they were nurses and doctors for the sick prelate. Bishop Worthington had a cast on his leg and a smile on his lips. Yes, I was surprised. His smile was unnecessary. They surrounded me. Jan pushed me against the cast on his brother's leg and the bishop pressed back. Hard plaster hurts. "Get up," he said. I did so. "Follow me." I did so. A steward drew a curtain and we had first class to ourselves.

"It's so easy for you to be our friend," Jan said. "Sit, please."

"And to be triply blessed," said the bishop. "You will be rich. You will be easy. You will be correct in what you do." He smiled a broad and clear celestial smile to make up for the earthly immobility of his leg. "And you will be alive. You would remain so. That is to be blessed in quadruplicate, I believe. Coffee with a lash of brandy, Sid?"

The first-class compartment was empty except for us. The steward removed himself. They had made their arrangements. Jan Worthington took a pear from the straw basket, and when he bit into it, a sweet jet of pear juice sprayed across the aisle. The pear was full to bursting with its juice.

From outer distance came commands to strap in, lift tables to upright position, extinguish cigarettes and smoking equipment . . . We are finding our cruising altitude through an unusual condition of cloud cover, nothing to worry about if you notice a change in the cabin pressure . . . The tune of motors changed and we were lifting off. Below, in the waters in which slaves and treasure had been deeped by storm or accident, I could see only a white sparkle on the ocean. Miami to Port-au-Prince now.

Jan said, "And so you will let go of Lucien, this madness of yours, and then we will generously and with Christian charity try you on another little job, a commodity this time, a less emotionally demanding commodity, a test of your attachment, my friend. We have been so disappointed."

"We hate to lose someone, Sid," said the bishop, "but we are close to losing you."

Lucien had looked puzzled, not terrified when I left him back in his seat. He was ready for whatever he had to do. Here in the belly of a 707, why should we quarrel with so much power?

"I'm not sure I'm ready for heroin smuggling," I said.

"Oh shush," said the bishop. "What makes you think you know what sort of commodity we may transfer? Such pride you have, my friend the mule. And perhaps it is something else and not narcotics at all, arms say, electronic equipment even, what might you comment in this event about your rash accusations?"

"I'd say I'm sorry. In that event."

"You would. Don't make us angry, Sid."

"Please," said Luci. "He already is."

"Ah Luci," said the bishop. "Always, always, always the characteristic feminine unclarity of your vision."

"You wouldn't know, would you, brother?" Jan asked.

Baskets of bananas, oranges, apples, purple grapes waited in little wicker containers on the table a few seats away. The steward came with a silver bucket and iced white wine. He poured. Then the first-class steward took himself elsewhere. It must have been planned that way. We were a team huddled in privacy. I was considering not about my safety but about the foolishness of self-esteem, this shadow of the pride I had given up. I caught myself relishing my advantages. I cared for someone, Lucien, not just Sid Kasdan and a fantasy recollection of a wife. Maybe I also loved the lad without desiring him and although we weren't even friends. Why else did I give myself to dragging him away from those who craved his body?

Lucien pulled the curtain and came into the compartment and sat. He was smiling and watching, looking very calm, his way when confused and anxious. Clever Lucien registered sleepy amusement, a Haitian invention which substitutes for an education.

I personally was ready to stop receiving insults, even from myself. I might offer them to others. I would stop merely reacting. I now chose to do for others—Lucien first, it seemed—and also for myself. I gave up hope of managing my life cleverly. Thank you, Luci and Worthingtons.

Wake up, Sid. The bishop was saying, "You have shown initiative in your foolish cause. We respect initiative; you need guidance in your causes. Some are intelligent in goals and some in their tactics. You are rather intelligent in your tactics, inventive, energetic, and—" he searched for another word in this thin dry stratospheric purity "—entertaining. In your goals, my dear friend, you are a fool."

He would not abuse me for the petty pleasure of it.

"But we can help to increase your efficiency. You need us."

Or he might abuse me for the deep pleasure of it.

"Of course, to destroy you for the inconvenience to which you have put us—you can understand how it frays our reputation among our clients in Palm Springs, and they communicate with Palm Beach, with Beverly Hills, with Paris and London and New York . . . No matter. We can handle that. We have a certain monopoly in our specialty, as you know . . ."

The bishop delivered a lecture which seemed intended partly to pass the time and partly to make something clear to himself. It had some of the character of a sermon. My attention was incomplete, despite the fact that he was talking about me.

"Sid, my lad, we do not despair," he was saying, "and you must not, either."

Prepare for landing. Extinguish your cigarettes and fasten your seatbelts. Nous approchons à l'île d'Haiti. Messieurs et dames, éteignez vos cigarettes s'il vous plaît ...

"Perhaps you had better come to the point," I said.

"You have a chance to survive," said the bishop. "Think of it as an opportunity which beckons you, Sid. You may live on. We have another proposal, but you must be very careful now not to distract us beyond repair." He squeezed my forearm and it hurt. His finger and thumb were strong. "I hope you can understand these simple statements."

"You haven't explained."

"I hope you learn to understand anyway, my friend and sometime colleague. Now scamper, please."

It's hard to think clearly while a plane is landing and a bishop is pinching. I thought this: Either they are just playing before hitting me hard or they really do want to give me a chance to come around before welcoming me onto home territory. It seemed they were not worrying about what I might want. But they may also have thought that my stretch of life with Lucien had educated me. A stretch of life sometimes changes the mind. A stretch of life with someone is a good means to alter intentions even if temperament remains the same. And even temperament is adjustable to facts, the bishop believed; otherwise, why follow a religion of exertion and will? And what had Lucien given me other than sleepiness?

From aloft, the island looked clean and sun-dried, shriveled like some giant raisin. Lucien murmured, "Home." I thought: Hope so. We landed. The Dieu Merci Papa Duvalier merengue band was playing on the airstrip, waving instruments and rattles and grinning their Welcome to Haiti Chéri. A dense crowd awaited our flight behind the concrete barriers, elegantly dressed Haitians, overheated white men in safari suits, a throng of porters and cab drivers and guides hoping for a buck. The expressions on their faces indicated they had not had much success in the past for this hope.

Suddenly police were pushing and shouting at us. Everyone made way for the police. The cops were wearing white t-shirts and blue jeans and wrap-around Acapulco sunglasses. I couldn't see their eyes, but I knew they were cops' eyes.

They wanted us out of the way of the cargo being unloaded from our flight. It did not go through customs. It was stenciled with the legend *LÉOPARDS CLUB DES SPORTS*—long wooden crates marked *Ping-Pong* (*Table Tennis*), and square crates marked *Clothing* (*Sweatshirts, Shorts*) and crates marked *Whiskey* (*Scotch*). Suddenly a man took me by the shoulder and asked, "What you look at, meester?"

I could see enough of his eyes to know he was not happy with me. He also managed to find the nerve that hurts in the elbow. I moved.

The Tontons Macoutes murderers, torturers, and extortionists of the days of Papa Doc had been phased out. Instead, Baby Doc encouraged a club of sportive Léopards who believed in physical fitness, the Revolution, and taking good care of enemies. A large notice under a photograph of the plump president-for-life stated:

> *My father the doctor François Duvalier,*
> *Inspirer of the People, made the political*
> *and culture revolution.*
> *We Jean-Claude Duvalier, President-for-Life,*
> *will make the economic and business revolution.*
> *Welcome to Haiti, Pearl of the Antilles.*
> *Carriers of weapons, narcotics, or subversive*
> *literature will be dealt with as they deserve.*
> > *J.-C. Duvalier,*
> > *President-for-Life*

A person in a starched white linen suit, a black skeleton with black pipestem limbs, took my arm. "Pass, pass, no

185

douane necessary, please. Bishop declare you are join with his party."

"Nothing to declare," I said, "no weapons, narcotics, or subversive literature."

"I have confidence," said the man in the white linen suit. "Such is the case. Bishop wish you a fine stay and see you one day very soon."

The eyes behind the glasses were invisible. The dense surge of the tropics was a wrapping for the heat which was upon me. It was the sweat of death upon me. I was frozen within moves that I had filled with vanity. I was encased in a slime of fear, and beneath that fear, which was only about murder, I cared not very much.

"Not very much," I said.

"Nothing at all to declare?" His teeth were bright and yellow; the membranes of his mouth were pink and wet.

"No."

"I thought you hear me. Pass. You also, the boy which come along." And the hilarious mask turned toward Lucien. "Since you are in the possession of this foolish blanc."

# Part III

**24** The white winter sun made a tropical place seem cold despite the droplets on my upper lip, the wet under my arms. The Hotel Oloffson, wooden towers balanced on the backs of termites, gave shelter to honeymooners, escapees from marriage, brinky revelers. My driver in his Mercury reject from Bogotá drove up the rutted driveway and stopped, sighing deeply to recover from his efforts, as if only his iron spirit had brought us alive through the teeming city. He arose, creaked open his door, creaked open ours, and stared at the blanc accompanied by the Haitian from abroad. He fell into silent tip-awaiting guard duty. A band, guitar, hand-pounded goatskin drum, and flute, broke into "Haiti Chérie" at the top of the winding stone staircase that led toward the iced, green, and salty drink offered by management to soothe the pangs of arrival. "La welcome, la welcome," said a cigar-smoking tourist, perking up from his week-old New York *Daily News*. "At last, I been waiting for some new blood here, sit down, tell me your story, you and your dusky friend. The name's Tony, the IRS calls me Anthony, I'm in waste disposal and sanitation—ecology, we call it—I'm buying the next one. You like these big rum fruity jobs?"

We moved by and I felt his hand touching my pants. Did he want to know if I had a weapon? Or was it merely a judgment about Lucien and me?

"We'll stay tonight, it's too late to get out of Port-au-Prince," I said to Lucien. "Tomorrow we end this phase."

"We finish the whole thing, yes?"

"Yes. The whole thing. This phase. Let's get to our rooms, get some sleep, and stay out of the way. Tomorrow you go home, Lucien."

A ninety-year-old porter scampered with our bags up the wooden ramp to the hotel annex where our rooms, once the maternity ward of a hospital, looked out over the city with its lamps, charcoal cooking fires, patches of electricity, and smoky patches of none. A sea-murmur swell of chicken, dog, and human noises washed back up the hill. The sub-squawk of automobile horns lay at the bottom of waves of sound. It was strangely soothing, a steady wall of noise on which I could build sleep or isolation in my thoughts. Lucien remained alongside. I stood at a wooden railing and stared out over the city. I too was not in a hurry to shut my door on this.

"Go to sleep," I said. This was the last night we would lie so strangely on twin beds in a hotel. It would be the last time we spent a night together.

"I am almost home," Lucien said, "so naturally now I will sleep, as you ask, as usual."

I walked back down the ramp to the bar. On the wooden terrace, early diners were eating by the flicker of oil lamps. Teachers here on charter flights, Haitian Air Force heroes in uniform, looking to detach some teacher or other from her companion, tropical boozers, elderly lady interior decorators with freckled bosoms in disarray with the hope of attracting a visiting earl or boozer or a Haitian Air Force hero, skinnied-out liver cases, fond of rum, a couple of pale, short-haired, long-toothed Marines who guarded the em-

190

bassy and referred to themselves as "personnel," a table of UNESCO or CARE bureaucrats in creaseless wash-and-wear.

I had a headache. The frontal lobe bulged and pressed against bone. Jet flights had unbalanced my cranial fluid. I wanted not to return to the room until Lucien was asleep. I didn't really need to protect him by sleeping in the same room, did I?

There was a familiar smell beneath the steady tropical hotel drench of flowers, sweat, rum, food—sharp light perfume coming from noplace, an aura. Dumb migraine aura. Dumb backsmell of memory far away here in Hispaniola.

My headache was trying to make further comment. Were all these lobby loungers what they seemed? The arrangement was too perfect. I wasn't sure they had spoken to each other before I arrived or would speak after I left.

I was dehydrated. I was a tired blossom myself. I asked for a fruit punch. It was too sweet. A Haitian captain came to my side and said softly, "Meester Sid. Do you wish now to return to your quarters?"

He was in silken khakis and an Eisenhower jacket. His red and blue epaulets were by Gilbert & Sullivan, Tailors. On his breast shone a medal from a twenty-year-old box of corn flakes. The face was more serious than the chest and the voice was unflirtatious and imperative. "Go back to your room. You need your rest, Meester Sid."

The band was chopping and sawing and plucking and singing at "Panama'm Tombé"—my Panama hat fell off—and bobbing and nodding at me. I thought I might as well do what everybody wanted me to do tonight, since I didn't have a really better idea. I had no plan other than to do what I wanted to do. The Haitian Air Force hero was treating me like a child with good reason.

I strolled up the little ramp that led to the annex where a bank of air conditioners, Fedders snouts all in a row, puffed and vibrated above the wooden slats of doors. My footsteps shook the open corridor. I was a few feet from my room when the neighboring door opened and the neighbor woman stood there. "Hi, Sid."

I would ride with this jolt. I would give her or anyone no satisfaction in my confusion. If I was chilled or heated, desirous or revulsed, dizzy all over, frightened, hopeful—there's the shameful thing—or all of the above, they were not to know. She must not know. The pit of my stomach squirms vividly for me, but I'll open no windows for others to look in. It's my anatomical secret. My squint at her nose, reddish and sunburnt it was, would be all she'd get. At present it was all I wanted to give.

"Don't you say hi when a person says hi, Sid? You used to be pretty free with your hi when you came through our door after a hard day checking on charter flights to Tiajuana or where the drooling transistor millionaire was hiding his cash—what you said you were doing, anyway. *Hard year at the office, Sid?* Say hi to a person, Sid."

I said, "What the hell you doing here?"

"It was a trip free of any charge."

"What are you to them?"

"Just your former wife is all. They asked if I'd visit you and I thought I'd better."

"Stop jiving and tell me."

"Won't you come in and we can discuss it comfortably? It's hot out here. You're trying to express too much with Baleful Stare Mark One."

"You wanted out of my life. You wanted me out of your life. This is not a game. It's not fair to practice your surprises on me."

"Did you hear my question, Sid? No strings attached, but the room is hotting up despite all that poor unit is trying to do. Please let's help out by you come in and we shut the door."

192

Lucien had known enough not to run away. If he left my side, he might be dead. He might be dead anyway. But I left his side with no tremor of doubt about taking my chances. I followed their moves and did what I wanted to do. Even if part of someone else's plan, as it surely was, someone who was not thinking of what was good for Sid, I would do this: I would follow my wife into her room. It was what in the world I most and only wanted to do.

"Shush. You're trembling," she said to me in the dark.

"It's only the vibration," I said.

**25** She shut the door and I asked, "Are they paying you?"

"Some," she said, "not too much by their standards, okay by mine—you never got me used to money, Sid—but they also threatened me."

"Mostly they persuaded you. Lots of money."

"Right. Have it your way. Persuaded and tax-free cash."

"You could have gone to the police. That was one of the alternatives for a practical person."

"They threatened *you*, Sid. I didn't know where you were. I didn't know if they would let you live if I went to the police." She let me chew on that awhile. "And then, from you, during our marriage, I learned a few things you taught me, such as do whatever you can yourself, without the salaried guardians of the peace."

"It's lonely out here."

"I learned it anyway."

And I digested that, too. After I had run it through my body, I remembered this lady rather clearly again. I asked, "What else do you want?"

"Now I'm afraid. I thought it would be more fun."

Such games. One thing which was always a minor factor in her life was being afraid. I asked, "Afraid of what?"

"A bad dream."

"How did you get all the way here? How did you know exactly when I'd show up? Did someone else make the arrangements? What records are there? Who back home knows you're in Haiti? Is there someone to come looking for you if you disappear? I can't take care of all these things without knowing."

"This time you can't anyway," she said. "It's all in the dream. Aren't you sleepy and don't you still like to drift?"

"Not lately," I said. "I'd prefer to wake up."

"Look at me carefully, don't avoid it," she said. "This time, Sid, there's no man I told how to find me."

"May I congratulate you on your rash of independence? May I present my compliments, madame? You look nice, Priscilla."

She was wearing a beaded band across her forehead. With her straight high-bridged nose I cannot in good conscience believe she hadn't figured on a charming Native American look from the late sixties, when Indians made a comeback. "What's that around your head? A headache?"

"No," she said sweetly, "you used to keep my brains together for me. Now I find a rag does it almost as well, better sometimes—a pretty rag."

How chic and cool of her to keep her dirty blond hair just dirty blond as god made it. How she didn't care what came, what life brought her, so long as it was just how she planned it. How she didn't know what her plans might be, but when they came she was sure of them. How negligent of care. How awful. How lovely she still was.

"Hello hello," she said, "you listening, dear?"

"I'm paying attention."

"I know you do that. I used to like that about you. But it doesn't mean you listen."

"You were saying I used to—"

"Hello hello I said after that." And then she asked, "Whatever possibly can this Lucian be for you that you run yourself into a maze with no good results at the end?"

"Luci*en*," I said, "nasalize it, it's French."

"I doubt if that's an answer to my question, but maybe. Their business is built on trust. Did you think they were going to let you get away with this, let Lu-ci*en* go home and tell the other boys they can sell themselves and then run away just as if they didn't make a deal?"

I shrugged. I was not concerned with their business anymore.

She looked into my eyes and shook her head and the beaded band flickered. "Sid, Sid, you never did think about the rules of what you get yourself into. People have conditions. Things have conditions, Sid. Oh Sid, grown man. Couldn't you just let things happen like they're supposed to?"

I stared. I would now do so.

"Okay, let's not just stand here. Do you mind sitting on a bed with me?"

It sagged. A strawlike smell came off mattress ticking sweated into by tourists. Romance takes funny forms, doesn't it?

"I've been wondering for years," I said. "Was there ever a time when you really did like me?"

"I remember."

"Can you be more specific? To me, it seemed you did, but please give date and details."

"I remember. Isn't that enough for you?"

"No."

"Well, what I didn't like was a tendency to ask if I loved you when you were just down and needed a lift—you just wanted to hitch a free ride—"

"Which was just when you didn't want to love me."

"Let me finish." She covered my large hand with her slim small one, a trick of hers. I had interrupted her and she frowned. "I guess I've finished," she said. "Specifically, what happened is not so much about you as about me. I remember how I waited for you to come home and how this frightened me, this waiting, that my happiness, so much happiness, depended entirely on you, Sid. This scared me, can't you understand?"

"Yes."

She smiled brightly. "So I did something about it."

Her kiss was fragile and abstract, the embrace of a woman who for years had seemed to be thinking of something she very much needed to do elsewhere, and yet my mouth found folds of meat and warmth, a humid desire within this abstraction. When I had been raw with her, I forced her to pay attention and she seemed to like this. When she screamed, it surprised us both. And I had loved her for it.

Time was passing since I first met Priscilla and the struggle was marking her. There was a tangle of veins on her thigh where she had been bruised or strained. When she would be seventy, a map of desolation here, if anyone cared to look. At eighty or ninety, if she lived, when some nurse turned her over in bed, what would the nurse see?

I, of course, would be charmingly dead. The body shreds and the mind is only one part of it. "What?" she asked.

I was singing softly the old song with which I used to tease her, Priscilla, Priscilla, she smells like vanilla, she keeps the mosquitoes away . . .

"Oh, no," she said.

"You're not sentimental," I said.

"I guess you know that about me. Anyway, I've been told—" Not sentimental, but funny; I used to think emotions had to come with the nice glint and laughter. She rubbed her cheek against mine. "I've been told, if this is ice-cream parlor time, I really taste more like sarsaparilla. Oh, oh, don't shoot up your eyebrows, it tickles. I taste myself sometimes. I keep fit for whatever the future may bring."

I thought: In the future, leave room for your own suffering.

I said: "I've been busy getting to unknow you, my dear."

"Does what you're doing now help? Since you used to think this—what you were doing awhile ago, Sid—got to know me?"

I had no answer for my clever lady. Through the slats came very little light. A microwave glow came from the heavily working innards of the air conditioner. I wondered if Lucien was asleep next door. I wondered if Priscilla and I were falling asleep together once more. A nice bed chat about ourselves and how we liked each other, and then once more falling asleep in each other's arms. I wondered if she had let the Worthingtons invite her on a trip because of me or because of her. Because of her—why? Because of me—why? Oh, whichever, it was nice to press my nose against her hair and breathe that light afterscent of love. It must be love from Priscilla because it smells like Priscilla's love. After awhile I slept.

I smelled rotting fish, barracuda, beached sharks in torn nets, machines for biting, and I awoke in the humid heat rising from the bay through the city. The air conditioner had snapped off during the night. I couldn't remember the rest of my dream. Obsession robs me of the real life of my dreams.

Long ago in San Francisco I dreamt that Priscilla was having her fingers done by a manicurist, and then I blinked awake to look at her fingers, and the nails were clear with clear polish, the cuticles neatly trimmed, halfmoons of white just where they were supposed to be. Waking Sid didn't notice she had taken to having her nails done, but sleep saw and made it a nightmare. I asked her the question. *Yes, she had taken a lover.* That power which robs us of the real life of our dreams is only doing it for our own good.

198

I stretched and yawned. A cock crowed crazily, all-day cocks they have there in Haiti, and dogs barking, donkeys braying, shoeshine boys cracking their boxes, children laughing, a turbulence of automobile brakes and horns. And in a white and silent space within all this noise, in a hotel enclave on a hillside, a woman, my wife, my former wife, my pale ex, *smells of vanilla*, said: "Hullo, friend."

"What are you doing here?"

"Hello again. Say hello."

"Repeat question."

"Working for the Worthingtons, they tempted me, Sid."

"How?"

"Said you were having fun."

"Why? Why? How did this happen?"

"Who can't use money and fun, friend?" she asked. "I was looking around. Nothing better to do. You might be glad to hear that. Nothing great going on. They said there was prosperity, travel, meet interesting people, sort of like the peacetime army—can't you understand that? I'm sure you do."

"What about me?"

"Might bug you a bit, I expect."

"I expect."

"That never stopped me, did it, Sid?"

She patted my thigh softly, a little congratulation for having the good sense not to answer this latest question.

"Hello again. Hello the third time. Hello there." She waited for me to smile, and when I didn't, she shrugged. That was my problem. "I got interested, friend. They interested me. Want to have breakfast? No, I guess it's too early. Wish I had a slice of pineapple, though."

"You're a remarkable person, Priscilla. I still don't understand you. Pineapple at dawn. You're a mystery to me."

I think I looked alert, but I know I didn't look for pineapple.

"How odd to find you in the slave trade," she said suddenly.

"I've considered that. Why me?"

Evidently the pineapple thought could be postponed. She smiled her wholesome, large-toothed, deceptively hilarious smile. "You were in the right place at the right time, my dear. It wasn't just luck. Right man for the job."

I shrugged. True; I am sometimes chosen.

"Everyone has a bad time. Everyone suffers. You don't believe this, but I have hard times, too. I've found life oppressive. That isn't slavery. What slavery is: is not being in possession of yourself. The Worthingtons knew what they were buying when they captured you."

I would listen. She used to say I didn't listen. I had never known anyone I wanted more to listen to.

"The interesting thing is how, in the end, they turned out to be wrong. You didn't stay captured. That interests me a lot, Sid. Thank you."

I spread my hands in my most Jewish bow. "De rien," I said.

"We'll see. I do rather like being interested by you, my dear."

I could think about slavery, I could think about pineapple, or I could think about her. Mine the choice. I wasn't free yet. "What happened to that fellow, that . . . tycoon?" I asked.

"Oh. I remember who you mean." Now it was her turn to shrug. "Sid. Dumb husband. The animals are stirring, aren't they?" She touched me with her long, warm, bony fingers.

"Oh lord. Oh lord."

"We mustn't unleash them, must we?"

"My dear."

"My old dear, too. We mustn't talk too much, must we? What you were doing was so much better."

She was busy over me. When had she practiced all this so perfectly? Did the tycoon give her lessons?

"No," I said.

"Yes," she said softly, "let me, of course let me, just let me, Sid."

My recent life had accustomed me to other people saying yes when I said no. I let her. If no good came of this, it probably didn't matter. Priscilla mattered.

"I'm here," she said, smiling in the glowing dawn. The air conditioner shuddered back into life and did its work.

"Are you ready to do a mother's job?"

"Is that what you want me to do? Just make you feel safe and comfortable?"

"I don't know anymore. Less lonely was what I used to want from my mother."

"Well, let's see, my dear. Psychic cuddling's not my line." As usual, she was crisp and efficient. Yet there might be gentleness there if a man could uncover it. Maybe I was right about that.

"Later that's what I wanted from you," I said.

"Less lonely?"

"Yes."

"Not really my line. Okay, I've waited," she said, "so now it's my turn to tell you things. You wanted so much sweetness, didn't you? Well, didn't *I*? You wanted all your dimensions, didn't you? Tough operator and little boy. Smart fellow and lonely child. Cuddle that frayed old Sid, right? Well, how about me? I wasn't a child anymore. I was tired of being just your dream girl. But I still had this kind of rough romantic soul you told me about, too. Maybe I even learned it from you."

"I let you down, Priscilla. That's made it so much worse."

"I didn't come here to nag. That's not my line, either, dear."

201

"No. We were both pretty silent for people who talk a lot."

We weren't now. We were mumbling away galeforce, top speed.

"Look. You see me hard now, don't you, Sid? It's true, I got hard. But somehow I got there by living with you—"

"I'm sorry."

"That's how I got to be thirty. A little foolish of me to blame you because I had a few birthdays. You see how human and petty I am? And now I'm even older than when I left you." I winced. "I know, I know, I really would have preferred you left me, but you were so stubborn. But now it's not all bad, Sid. I'm also here. They said you were going to die. They said I had a chance to save you. They didn't exactly say, but it seemed clear enough. I wanted to see you. I wanted you to touch me. So I'm here."

The dream about barracuda was wrong. How could I be so angry with her when I loved her so much? Her smile was full of teeth, but that was laughter in it, not biting.

"You shouldn't make anything special of this."

"You always say that."

"Okay, I have my own way about things. But I'm glad I'm here, Sid."

I remembered her while she kissed my forehead. She ran her lips over furrows. She was trying to smooth. She was trying to close my eyes with kisses. She had been disappointed in love, too. She was trying to recruit me into riding, eyes closed, just riding with the dream we had once shared, like two kids on a beach, plugged into the same transistor radio.

"Why are you smiling?" she asked.

"I don't know."

"Okay, don't tell me, but stop it. Just drift. Just go with it. Please, Sid. Pretend you're sleeping and I'm just doing this while you sleep."

I let her ride. She had her way. I dreamt I was sitting on top of a train which was about to enter a tunnel. I saw the tunnel and I didn't see it, and I was about to lose my head. How goddamn different is that from the barracuda dream? Then I woke up, not because my dreams are boring, which they are because they are mostly about me, but because someone was shaking me.

Priscilla was gone. I opened my eyes but didn't make any sudden move. This much of me was still professional. Lucien was shaking me awake.

**26** He stood aside, watching me. The door was open. I wrapped a towel around my middle and went out onto the ramp to look down the hill to Port-au-Prince. Lucien said nothing and returned to his room. I inhaled the morning; tried to loosen my chest. I would come alive in due course.

I had gotten used to this blanket of sound, this negative silence of animal yelps and howls, chicken caws, automobiles with mufflers gone, babies crying, transistor radios squeaking Latin music or the merengue, kids tapping on cans, boxes, drums. Every few milliseconds, a dog grew oppressed by all the stillness, therefore barked into it and scared a matted-haired burro or donkey or goat and it started again. If a man was beating his wife to death, you might miss it in the negative silence. If a man was beating another man to death, you would have to cup your hand over your ear to pick up the details.

There were people jerking along down the hillside road below. Nobody was killing anybody just yet, so far as the eye could see. The ear tended to contradict this. I heard a great rising howl of marital strife, screaming followed by laughter.

People in Haiti are not death freaks like some I know in California. They don't kill each other silently, or make love silently, even when the children are standing around with eyes shining, learning the lesson. They die and fuck noisily. Priscilla had come silently down to the Caribbean to accompany me on a small inch of my voyage with Lucien. But now where had she gone (to whom)?

I went back inside and shut my door. I knew what this could lead to. As soon as I was alone, I would have company. They waited for that. Lucien would return immediately.

Knock-knock. Not a joke. Knock-knock-knock.

"Hold a sec," I said.

This is my mind working, trying to work and what I remember is that marked-down label: *Hold a sec.* I knew this mayhem would be over soon, and it would end with mayhem.

I was far retreated inside my head. One step at a time was all I could take; one step forward for Lucien, eleven steps backward into old and tangled needs. Priscilla. Luci. The Worthingtons. And me on leave from reality. On sleepless jobs, long ago, I had learned to use speed, and then learned it was worth punching myself in the face to keep awake rather than do that again. My head was back in those volcanic disturbances of sense. An island was floating in the sea and I was at the dead root of it. Bleeding ooze. Frozen lava. *Wait a sec.* I said I would open the door and I did.

"Meester. Meester."

"You don't talk pidgin, Lucien. And you don't keep disappearing."

"My friend, what we do? I am frightened, also."

"Don't you remember you were scared in California? You got unfrightened over the rest of America. You fell asleep for three thousand miles."

"Here at home I am real to me," he said.

"Who were you there? Was that a corpse I was dragging?"

"If I die in California, I just disappear. If I die in Haiti, I am a ghost."

This was a local point I could not argue very well.

"And you also will be a ghost here. They have power in this country, more than elsewhere. They have all the power."

The distinctions in his mind did not fit the case perfectly. All the power was not theirs; I knew that. But they had enough to kill him, to kill me, and that was sufficient as far as I was concerned. I wanted very much to hang around for the rest of what would happen to me. Priscilla had opened a door and walked out, but she had left the door open. I liked surprises again. Good. I also liked administering them to others.

"Lucien," I said, "I want you very fast now, quick, to get ready and we're going to Kenscoff. I want you home, out, away, I want to be free of you, *now get ready*. We're going."

"I understand," he said.

"Do it."

And then I'll slide on a slimy slug and break my neck.

"I will do whatever you say."

"Thank you very much. Go."

"Because it makes no difference anymore."

I turned to him. There was a rustle under my bed, like the echo of an earthquake. Lucien was not finished with saying he would do whatever I asked. He uttered in a shrill hiss the words stuck in his throat all across America: "You did this for yourself. Not for me. You did it for yourself!"

"You think so. Stipulate that. Isn't that what people do?"

"Stip-u-late," he repeated. "Worse, worse! You also did it for me."

206

"My friend, now I don't understand you."

"Because," he said, putting his face very close to mine, smiling so that I could feel his warm breath on me, a warmth and odor of rapid combustion, a stench of fever, "because you would not have done it otherwise."

"Otherwise what?"

"Otherwise you would not. You did it for me, too, because I am mignon." He made that juicy Haitian kissing noise at me, that hot cocoa mix noise through the air. "Because you like me so much that way, meester, you do not know how—"

I hit him and he went down against the bed. The damp smell of the mattress in Priscilla's room was flailed into the air. I said *cute* to myself. I didn't remember hitting him, but I watched him fall and I felt the sharp pain in my hand. I was caressing my knuckles.

"It changes nothing," he said. "You even want to bloody me. You took me from a man who stuck me behind for his pleasure. And you are a man who hits me near the mouth for your pleasure."

From under the bed a rat scurried with a mouthful of mango rind. It disappeared into a hole in the opposite wall. This was its route from the kitchen, a transfer of rot, serving its nest. Lucien watched me watch the rat. He smiled. There was a thick untended trickle from the cut on his face. He began to unbutton his shirt.

"Don't do that," I said.

He used the tail of the shirt to wipe his face. He was still smiling. I had thought he was unbuttoning his shirt to receive me. And then he began to unhook his belt.

"Stop it!"

While we stood there and he seemed to be thinking whether to do what I said, obey me like a slave, or do what the Worthingtons had hired him to do, service white men, like a slave, there came a knock at the door. We stood there

207

listening, two friends modestly dressing together after a nap. The knock was soft and steady. It was not loud. It was all we could hear.

"Qui est là?" I said.

"Old friend."

It was Mahmoud, dressed in a white linen suit, looking thick and tall, and at home. His sunglasses were folded into his pocket behind the blue silk handkerchief. "M. Fils-Aimé," he said.

"I remember you."

"I am alone," he said.

"Why are you here? What are you looking for?"

"I am alone because I am sufficient to the task," he said. He looked at Lucien, partly dressed Lucien, and grinned. "Our business is built on trust, you understand now?"

Those were the same words Priscilla had used.

I began to push him back through the open door. He stopped the door with his foot and kicked it shut. I shoved him sharply, but he had a surprising agility and leverage. "Please," he said, "one moment." And he hit me in the mouth with his fist. I coughed against the tooth I swallowed, a thick small smooth bone with one jagged edge. I was busy breathing, arranging my throat for breathing, and did not remember falling. I was climbing up very slowly as he stood over me, waiting while I coughed and coughed at my tooth. He was wearing the white suit over a Léopards sport costume. He was wearing blue-striped white jogging shoes. He began to pull his umbrella out of its case (it's not raining, I thought) while he watched me choke at the tooth in my throat. I could feel it turning with a broken root scraping from within. I could feel my own blood rushing from the spot to grease its way. The umbrella Mahmoud pulled from its case was not an umbrella; it was a cane; it was not a cane; it was a sword cane and Lucien just stood up and stretched his body to greet it. "In the French fashion," said Lucien, "if I had a glass, I would like to drink—"

"It was not part of your agreement," said Mahmoud. "S'il te plaît, Lucien." And he stabbed Lucien very smartly in the chest. A thickness bubbled from the unbuttoned shirt. Lucien said nothing more, he smiled; blood percolated from the hole, and then it gushed from his mouth and Lucien fell.

Mahmoud bent over to gaze at the results. There was contempt in this. He turned from me, knowing I had not acted and would not act. I hit him on the back of the neck and he tumbled without a word. I bent to Lucien and ripped open his shirt. No. His eyes on mine smiled. A dimness swept over them. I brushed the eyelids shut.

I stood over Mahmoud. He was breathing shallowly, with a kind of crepitating hoarseness, like a shorted-out radio dial; first I heard it, then didn't, then did again. There was a knock at the door of the room. "Nobody here!" I shouted. The door wasn't even locked. The man didn't try the door. I heard footsteps padding away. Adidas or tennis shoes, like Mahmoud's.

He was still alive. I stood over him with his sword raised where I could drive an edge into him. The tip was as sharp as a razor. It was stained with Lucien. I did not call for a doctor. I did not use the sword.

I thought now of going for the Worthingtons.

To bring Lucien home from that veterinarian's house in Palm Springs had brought him to death by a sword in the chest, it had brought Mahmoud Fils-Aimé to a broken neck and choking on his blood, it had brought me to these sleepy murders. It had brought me to the Worthingtons. I opened the door to the long sloping wooden hallway outside, open to the hillside and the noises and lights, electric glow and charcoal fires of Port-au-Prince. Whoever had knocked had gone. I waited here with the door open to see who might come for me and what I would do for Mahmoud when he

209

woke up. This interested me. He snored like a man in peaceful sleep, with a disturbed sinus and a callus in his throat.

The body of Lucien, beside which I waited—I did not kneel—was that of a small manliness erased. A child lay there with purplish skin. Fate had changed its mind about a pretty boy. My face felt frozen and stiff. I remembered this feeling when Priscilla said she wanted free of me. Lucien had also gotten free. An ache of pain knocked through my body, seeking to get out, battering my ribs, as if my flesh had been exhausted by the hiccupping sobs of childhood. And he was cold now. In this hot climate men turned as cold as death elsewhere. A mosquito buzzed over his eyelids and disappeared, uninterested.

I couldn't hide in Haiti. I couldn't hide here. Among the dead and the alive, the visible and invisible, I was white and evident and at the end of running. Maybe Priscilla had not come to join me; maybe she had only come to see what the Worthingtons wanted to show her, a showboating trip at their request, for their purposes about me.

No. She meant something more; I was sure of that. I could fail, but how could Priscilla fail? I very much wished to earn enough life more to find an answer to this question. Priscilla had designed herself to get what she wanted.

Mahmoud was groaning. He was fluttering his eyes and trying to push the mosquito away from his nostrils.

I felt the empty place where my tooth had been. I lifted a clot of blood with my tongue and the socket felt strangely clean. Time to lose one, I suppose. Root canal work had postponed this day. I had pretended to remain young, with a full mouth of teeth.

"Don't point my umbrella at me," Mahmoud whispered, smiling.

But I wasn't pointing it. I was merely holding it.

"If it penetrates, it will hurt. I try to make noise."

"It will surely kill you first."

He liked to discuss. The *délire verbal* of Haitians. He was at his ease with broken bones in his neck. He grimaced, but could wait for developments. Perhaps later he could move. He tried to spit; blood dripped at the corners of his mouth.

"Someone will come," he said hoarsely. "You may kill me or you may leave me like this. In either case, you will not like the Caserne. Or the prison. Our police, our army, our Léopards—you remember the Macoutes? Yes, of course, that was very bad, so now instead we have the Léopard Sporting Club, of which I am captain. In our Caserne, sir, men drink urine and eat what they should not eat. They are urged to perform certain tasks. They are hurt by other men. Ah, perhaps you would like that. They beg to die. My friend, you will envy Lucien."

"I've thought about that."

"Already?"

"Many times."

"Do you care what happens to your wife?"

"Former wife," I said.

"Ah." He was sweating. There were little mucusy beads on his lip. He moved his elbows behind him, trying to lift himself a bit, or to see if he could lift himself, but he didn't find the answer to this question, because I held the umbrella to his neck. He fell back, perhaps relieved not to make an effort that gave him pain. From where he lay, Mahmoud yawned and then stretched his lips. The yawn was catching; the grimace was not. The bones of my neck were intact. A man lying there at my mercy, a murderer who had made the intention of my life meaningless, could still infect me with his yawn. He had infected me with killing. I had also been infected with my wife's wishes, and wriggled, and did not wriggle free.

Mahmoud had a little speech he wanted to make. "People say we are the worst in the world for prisons. Oh, or perhaps as good as the Syrians. But who is to say whether in the case of criminals the worst is not the best? Has the theory been fully tested and explored? I ask, who is to judge?"

"You're very worldly for a guide—"

"*Chauffeur*-guide. We have a French education in our country. In my position one must absolutely read and write." He stretched his lips again in a smile. He too found it odd to give a lecture on Haitian pedagogy with a sword umbrella at his throat. "I have several talents, sir, including to live. I don't need to die, my friend—do you? Meester Sid, do you absolutely require torture in order to fulfill your destiny, and then to die unlamented, even by yourself?"

It was a complicated question. I considered some of it. Mahmoud Fils-Aimé needed to die. I felt sure of this. I raised the sword slightly, for the distance it would travel would ease his suffering. His eyes followed mine with that wooing look which Lucien also had offered me in moments of confusion. If I had a chance, I would grieve for Lucien. If I could live long enough, I would. I moved the point down to measure the distance. I felt the tightness of his skin transmitted like a drum vibration through the tip of the sword. "Oh, that hurts," he said, "you don't realize how it hurts."

I should finish him with a knife or a gun. I disliked this weapon he had pressed on me. He was breathing hoarsely, with fright, with the injury I had given him, like an accident victim, but his mind controlled through the shock. He was even amused by my indecision. I was having difficulties. Mahmoud could not help me very much.

He gazed down his nose at the sword. "You will have the devil of a time cleaning it," he said. "My blood tends to stain."

"That won't be necessary," I said. "I'm not tidy."

"Are we not nice friends now, just talking and joking like this?"

"No," I said.

I waited while his breathing came around. I did not want to kill him while he was pumped with phlegm and adrenalin and words. I wanted him to appreciate what we were doing together. I had little choice. Lucien lay with his eyes closed by my fingers and the mosquito that bothered me would not bother him.

The prospect of my own death was almost trivial to me. This man, Mahmoud: I could hurt him when necessary, but I had difficulty passing the final judgment on him. If I thought about torture, about what the Worthingtons or the Macoutes or the Léopards might do to me, about Priscilla, I could also learn to kill him. I was thinking of these things. I was waiting and his eyes followed my thoughts. He was pleased that I took this moment for pensiveness.

Gradually his breathing became steady. He seemed to decide it was best not to move, and he was correct in this belief. I stood over him while he relaxed. Haitians learn to nap when they can. His red-rimmed, white-rimmed eyes were wide. He watched. He was curious about what I might do next. So was I. Spectators are found everywhere, and especially where death is one of the stakes in the game.

I was interested in what I would do next. I was anxious to learn.

There was a peppery smell of sex in the room. He had taken his pleasure when I hit him. He enjoyed the hanged man reflex without being hanged. Something snapped in his neck. I was not dead yet, either. He stared. He was, it seemed, at peace. And as long as I spent my time thinking of what to do with him, I did not have to think of Lucien, that object lying there on the floor behind him.

He looked a little like Lucien.

I called the hotel desk. They called the police. But it was Bishop Worthington, not the Haitian police, who came to hear my confession.

He stood at the open door in his robes, black and red, for mourning, I suppose; with no jewelry around his neck, so as not to implicate his god, I suppose. He was smiling. His teeth were bright, regular, small, a well-bred girl's teeth. The skin of his neck was roughened by too much sun, but his face was pink and glowing. He did not shut the door. He did not require privacy in this place, which belonged to him. He barely glanced at Mahmoud, who stared at him without speaking. Mahmoud knew it would not be important enough to him to ask for help.

Across the ramp, down the hill, beyond the crowned palms with their claylike crust on the trunks, the smoky haze of late morning arose from the city. A shoeshine boy was passing below, beating his wooden box. "Vot secretai! Netoyé chausseu! À vot se'vice!"

"Sid, it's time now. You've been willful, Sid."

"Yes, sir."

"Do you regret this? Are you sincerely sorry?"

"No."

"Are you willing to pretend?"

"No."

"Do you wish to live?"

"Could be."

"You're not very logical in your thoughts for a person with a keen logical mind, Sid."

I had no answer for this. My wife was still with me in some way. She still wanted something from me. She still saw her shadow somehow connected with mine. For this, she needed that my shadow still be cast by the sun against my body. The details were hidden by the intentions of others. Of Priscilla. Of the Worthingtons. There was too much light around here and I couldn't see. But she still wanted to give me back my life, what I hadn't been able to do for Lucien.

Shadows sometimes lack very important details, don't they? I still wanted everything from her.

"Where is she?" I asked. "What does she want from this?"

"What do we want from dear Priscilla is how the question should be framed, dear Sid."

"Okay," I said. "I guess I'd prefer to hang out awhile."

"You've been a difficult lad. What can we still get from you is the rest of the correct question."

I said nothing. This was a difficult interview. Heat tends to make me nervous unless I keep moving.

"I'm concerned about you, Sid. It's not really a personal matter. You must work out a keen logical reason, dear colleague, why you should evade our righteous justice. Why you shouldn't be dumped into a ravine like a sick chicken—" he shrugged and the robes rippled on his shoulders "—an unnecessary baby."

"Vot secretai! À vot se'vice!" A puff of darker charcoal smoke appeared from the caille-paille, a lean-to of banana leaves and packing crates, down the slope from the hotel ramp. Allis-Chalmers. Maison Electra. "I'd prefer to negotiate," I said.

"Ah, Sid."

"I said I'd like to work something out. Don't push me too far."

He was smiling. He had a well-bred girl's gleam in his smile, and his eyes were smiling, too. But they were also figuring if I could still be used and if I could be controlled. If it would be worth trying to control me. If I was controllable.

"You will have to suffer, Sid."

"Yes."

"People who get what they want must suffer for it, Sid."

"I know that."

"You know that *now*, Sid."

I looked at him, wondering if he too felt pain for what he wanted. But it would be rude to inquire. The smile would flicker out, and all in all, although I didn't like his smile, I preferred it to his not smiling.

"Are we ready to move?" I asked.